My Beautiful Bus

MY

BEAUTIFUL

BUS

By Jacques Jouet
Translated by Eric Lamb

DALKEY ARCHIVE PRESS

CHAMPAIGN / DUBLIN / LONDON

Originally published in French as *Mon bel autocar* by Editions P.O.L, Paris, 2003

Library of Congress Cataloging-in-Publication Data
Jouet, Jacques.
[Mon bel autocar. English]
My beautiful bus / Jacques Jouet ; translated by Eric Lamb. -- 1st ed.
p. cm.
"Originally published in French as Mon bel autocar by Editions POL, Paris, 2003."
ISBN 978-1-56478-799-6 (pbk. : alk. paper)
I. Lamb, Eric. II. Title.
PQ2670.O926M6513 2013
843'.914--dc23
2012033339

Cet ouvrage a bénéficié du soutien des Programmes d'aide à la publication
de l'Institut français/ministère français des affaires étrangères et européennes

This work was supported by the Publications Assistance Programs of the French Institute /
French Ministry of Foreign and European Affairs

The publisher acknowledges the financial assistance of
Ireland Literature Exchange (translation fund), Dublin, Ireland.

www.irelandliterature.com
info@irelandliterature.com

Partially funded by a grant from the Illinois Arts Council,
a state agency

www.dalkeyarchive.com

Cover: design and composition by Mikhail Iliatov

Printed on permanent/durable acid-free paper and bound in the
United States of America

The mother won't tell her daughter the end.

CONTENTS

If it so happened that I had to decide, among the legible world's variety of propositions, or more specifically among those candidates under the category of road signs, which legible suggestion deserves to be called the most counter-logical and disarming, then it turns out I wouldn't have much trouble.

It isn't unusual to discover, along roads of all sorts, this odd triangular image that the authorities have erected in plain view—

—signaling a crossing for aroused deer running at full speed, which drivers must avoid hitting, even though everyone knows that at such locations the average driver will hardly ever see the slightest trace of one.

On the other hand, I've never come across a sign like this one—

NO

DUMPING

—which doesn't seem to have compensated for its absence of images with the inevitable reality lying below it, a pile of trash, foodmechanical waste, debris, and printed material, which no longer signify by themselves, a sort of illiterate provocation aimed at overly abstract or arbitrary prohibitions.

For my part, if I've announced anything on the cover of my book that won't actually appear in these pages, it can only be my name—and not just my name, but also the possessive pronoun modifying the bus . . . as if I hadn't recalled Pascal:

Certain authors, speaking of their works, say, "My book," "My commentary," "My history," etc. They resemble middle-class people who have a house of their own, and always have "My house" on their tongue. They would do better to say: "Our book," "Our commentary," "Our history," etc., because there is in them usually more of other people's than their own.[1]

_____

[1]Pascal, Blaise. *Thoughts,* from *The Harvard Classics*, New York: P.F. Collier & Son, 1909-1917. "Thought # 43." Translated by W. F. Trotter.

On the contrary, what have I *not* put on this cover that may indeed appear in these pages? That's my first question. And for the reader who reads only the warning labels and then puts the book aside, well, that's too bad. This book won't be the one that garners more than my normal share of five hundred readers or earns royalties beyond my advance.

I supplied the label "novel" reluctantly. Even though writers have only recently been expected to give their books these labels, I'm naïve enough to be proud of my denial of this new practice. The reason is simple: I'm searching for a new form for narrative. In it, fiction will be the object of a conquest, a campaign in which the reader will be enlisted, though first he'll be asked to endure a few pages of training, explanations of story and strategy.

Who wouldn't enjoy slipping into the imaginative tale? One moment you aren't there yet (just as when, not so long ago, you'd have to wait through newsreels and cartoons at the movie theater), and the next you're right in the middle of it. Are you there yet?—Well, if I'm not, then please put me there. And if I'm in too deep, please come and join me, to share the experience or pull me out.

We aren't looking for fiction, but rather the search for fiction. When fiction is too commandeering, it becomes nothing but mere brutality. Continuous fiction is boring. The chase is better than the catch.

They do not know that it is the chase, and not the quarry, which they seek.[2]

---

[2]Pascal, "Thought # 139"

At this point, the story will follow some paths that may appear whimsical on the surface. It will follow changes in the landscape and the seasons. A closer look will reveal that the narrative is, in fact, rigorously following logical paths that it is unaware of, or that the current page is hiding.

What do the Republic's road-maintenance crews dream of while hunched over their tools? They dream of dreams. And what other things do the ticket inspectors and the mechanics dream of? And what about the bus drivers? Bus drivers—and their passengers—dream of buses, or of anything else that their vehicles' attributes allow. And if they always dream of a more beautiful bus, then at least one example in particular must be the starting point, and more precisely the closest one—their own. Or maybe they dream about who owns the rows of crops they see through its windows.

My beautiful bus is in its garage in Châtillon, a garage that suits its dimensions perfectly. There isn't enough space for two like it. It's sheltered. It doesn't sleep on its side.

The driver of this beautiful bus is sleeping in a nearby hotel room. The Levant hotel has only six rooms, each one of them modest. On the wallpaper, a team of white horses repeats itself. There's a light bulb on the ceiling, in a glass globe, and a little neon light on the bedside table. The man takes up one half of a double bed. The right half remains empty, reserved for an absent companion. He sleeps in pajamas, with one arm covering his face, his nose wedged in the fold of his arm. He swallows continuously, as if he were dry-mouthed, thirsting for a drink.

An electronic alarm clock on the bedside table goes off at six o'clock, as it had been set to do. A few seconds later, in turn, the nearby church strikes six long notes. Why doesn't the town hall sound its bell?

The driver uses Basile as his only name, and is twenty-five years into his career. He doesn't live in Châtillon, but in a town eighty kilometers away, somewhere along the national highway. Every time he drives by his own quaint little house, he honks as a sort of hello to his wife, their daughter, the cat, and his garden gnomes.

Basile has slept in Châtillon on his company's dime, as he does each time he gets in late and needs to leave again at dawn.

A trip home would add too many kilometers and drastically diminish the day's profits to a break-even outcome. When work is scarce, you do what you need to do.

During these nights, Basile continues to drive in his sleep. In the morning, upon waking, he intently makes his way to the bathroom. He keeps his eyes closed for as long as possible. Basile washes himself from head to toe. He opens his eyes. He shaves and brushes his teeth. Once showered, he rediscovers his face in the mirror. He rediscovers his name, and then his wife's: Odile. He slips into his overalls. He folds the alarm clock into his pajamas and packs everything in a travel bag.

Between the hotel and the garage, hardly 200 meters by foot, Basile doesn't see the least bit of Châtillon, not a soul among its thousand or so inhabitants. He doesn't notice its 900-meter elevation, its ruins of a Templar stronghold, or the second-rate RV campground . . . He's thinking through the things he has to take care of before the departure, his routine.

Basile pampers the beautiful bus before departing. It rained yesterday and the lane-expansion project on the highway made for a muddy trip. There hadn't been any triangular road signs carrying the inscription MUD, which would have been spelled out of course, since a graphic depicting mud doesn't exist.

My beautiful bus is two-and-a-half years old. It's a hardy vehicle that Basile himself has tamed. It's a VH 300 with a standard wheelbase, forty-nine non-adjustable seats plus the driver's (the nine folding seats were taken out), a six-cylinder engine, a passenger door, a lateral exit, and luggage compartments on each side. It's equipped with hydraulic power steering.

My beautiful bus is lavender blue with white stripes. Its sunshades are the same faded blue. On winter mornings its exhaust is sometimes blue.

Relatively speaking, the bus driver is older than his vehicle. He's only eight years away from retirement, and his increasingly frequent medical checkups yield healthy results: they've been checking his heart, reflexes, sight, and hearing.

When Basile, who's an early riser, is at last prepared for all the eventualities imaginable in his line of work, he attends to his vehicle. In the garage, the bucket sits in its place under the faucet, and the rags sit in theirs, as well as the paper towels and the sprinkler head, which is attached to a hollow metal broom handle . . . The parts of the bus that Basile cleans: the windshield, the headlights, the taillights, the mirrors, the luggage compartment handles, and the passenger windows. What Basile polishes: the steering wheel. What Basile changes from time to time: the headrest covers.

The tires—the air pressure and wear—and the brakes are checked regularly . . . Basile takes to his job with the required sense of responsibility. He doesn't abandon his role as a link between citizens. He doesn't talk about things he doesn't know about. A driver who doesn't reach beyond his pedals!

When I first started dealing with Basile and the beautiful bus, I was discouraged because I wasn't sure what to make them dream about, as if I hadn't consulted Perrault: no matter how it looks, we shouldn't move from the story toward morals, nor should we sneak from morals toward the story, rather, we should progress from openly self-conscious reflection toward the invented story, with provocation as its only end: a story is unique, it generally has nothing to show, nothing to represent, other than what could *potentially* be real.

The word, the world . . .

When you speak of the *wolf*, you see its tail . . . In this case, language affirms its power to pull the hood off something, and affirms its skill in uncovering what convention has inadvertently stashed away, enhancing the meaning with warmth and sarcasm, if we're dealing with literature. However, it shouldn't be forgotten that in certain highly contradictory hotels, boiling hot water won't come out of the faucet unless you turn the blue knob, a cold color. It shouldn't be forgotten that in the reader's apartment, which the author has asked to enter, the author believes that he wields all the power (including the power to gain the complicity of the reader, for which the latter isn't even awarded a discount on the visit and the thin volume left behind). In the majority of cases, the author takes this power for granted.

If the wolf's malicious paw must be forgiven just a little, and the listener fooled to however small a degree—just as Puss in Boots plays dead to catch mice—then it would be helpful to look to Perrault first, to read and reread *Puss in Boots*, and, before saying a word, to carefully mull over the delightful formula:

"Here you are, sire, a cottontail rabbit . . ."

Puss in Boots is not a cat. He would have four boots if he were a cat. Puss in Boots is the author of an adventure, and it may well be that the narrative cat's got his tongue for the rest of his life.

Let's sum the story up.

Times are tough, and the setting is a mill in the impoverished countryside. The miller dies, leaving behind three children. The eldest and the middle child band together to secure inheritance of the means of production and trade—the mill and the donkey. But the least fortunate of the three heirs, the youngest, is left to starve, day in, day out.

As each day fails to satiate him, he remembers the previous evening's brewing hunger; he's still hungry for the following day, and the day after that, and so on until eternity. Even if he were to skin and eat his whole inheritance, a cat, he would still be hungry. That cat, Puss in Boots, swings a satchel over his shoulder, puts boots on his feet, and sets off on a hunt. He tricks a rabbit into his trap.

. . . pulling the strings immediately, he caught it and killed it without mercy.

Proud of his catch, he headed to the king's estate and asked to speak with him. He was brought up to His Majesty's chamber where, having entered, he bowed graciously to the king and said to him:

"Here you are, sire, a cottontail rabbit [. . .]"

At this point, *Puss in Boots* inverts the "natural" logic of the narrative (the future Carabas is hungry; the rabbit should have gone straight to him), which numerous manipulations of the story—a temptation to which too many pen-pushers and editors have succumbed—rush to modify at this precise point in

18

Perrault's text. Among the manipulators, many tend to fill in the blanks strategically put in place by Perrault's use of the ellipsis:

Surely you are thinking that the cat will hurriedly bounce home to his master and bring him his catch. But here, you are completely mistaken. Our hunter had other plans, and it wasn't toward his master's little cottage that he was headed.

(*Puss in Boots,* from Perrault, ed. Hemma, Paris, 1956.)

Here's a second example among the many appalling modifications:

"I am going to go for a jaunt in the woods. Wait for me, master."
When the cat returns a few moments later:
"Look, master. I have caught a beautiful rabbit."
"What shall we do? Eat it?"
"Why no, master. I will now bring it to the king."

(*Le Chat Botté,* livre-disque, Touret, 1977.)

In this third example, it's carefully made known that first and foremost the king is a gourmet:

He swung his bag over his shoulder and headed toward the royal castle, for he had heard that the king had a vice for rabbit pâté.

(*Le Chat botté,* éd. Fernand Nathan, Paris, 1974, images et texte de Jacques Galan.)

All of these dubious manipulations attempt to spare the reader—and the fact that the proverbial reader is a child is no excuse—from a confusing twist that is supposedly beyond his grasp. However, it's at this precise moment that the story winds through a surprise acceleration, which is the master stroke of a masterpiece. The same narrative craftiness predates Perrault in *Facetious Nights* by the Italian storyteller Straparola, in which the primordial Puss in Boots can be found.[3] But this tale is more diluted on the whole. By contrast, Perrault delivers the story with a brisk, irrefutable stroke of the pen. And here we find what Master Charles masters: insinuation, relaxation, patience, and rhythm.

It's very clear to me that this subtle jostling of the reader and his lazy habits is one of the secrets behind a beautiful story. Perrault catches up to Pascal on this point: trickery and strategy are more powerful than the cottontail rabbit itself, which is in no way useful in the practical sense (even if it does turn out that the king delights in a dish of rabbit pâté, presumably that's not a luxury or a rare delicacy for him), but rather which acts as a testimony, from one hunter to another, of an equality of privileges, sets the rise of a future nobleman off to a good start, and leads to a climb in social standing by the main character, which is one of the story's themes.

Following the advice of his John-the-Baptist cat, the youngest and most miserable of the heirs—you and me, or, in other words, us—who doesn't even have a Christian name, undresses and dives into the river. As soon as he emerges from its depths, he becomes the newly christened Carabas, who climbs into a carriage,

---

[3]"The First Fable: Costantino Fortunato," recounted by Fleurdiane during the Eleventh Night: *Les Facecieuses Nuictz* by Giovanni Francesco Straparola, London, 1901, translated from Italian into English by W. G. Waters.

dressed differently, and rides through the countryside collecting fruits and grains, wrenched with the help of repeated blackmail from the mouths of working peasants cowed by Puss in Boots's warning that he will dice them up into pâté.

In *Memoirs of My Life*, Charles Perrault boasts about having been instrumental in convincing the gentlemen from Port-Royal to see the importance of directly addressing the public outside the Sorbonne in order to keep them informed of the Jansenist-Jesuit dispute. "The First Letter Written to a Provincial by One of His Friends" came as a result of this advice, and was followed by seventeen others, written by an anonymous, progressive Pascal. Which leads me—straddling seven leagues in a single stride, and this time allowing Pascal to catch up to Perrault—to compare and mix together, as a mortar for my verbal construction site, five-shilling coaches and char-à-bancs.

In this letter, Blaise Pascal, with the help of his childhood friend Artus de Roannez and some others, conceives the democratic vision of a Parisian omnibus, even though he, like everyone else, had always ridden on coaches, the bus rides of the *Grand Siècle* that covered the expanses of land and water between Clermont and Paris—Pascal, who is unable to extinguish his ambition and inventiveness, who accuses Aristotle and the prophets of double standards in the vast yet confined space where he may contradict authority, who is unmatched as he discovers and fires and forges the sentences of his logical proofs, so many of which have entered into the French language (there are times when it's appropriate to call Pascal Pascal, and others where it's more fitting to call him the Master Wordsmith), and to such a degree that he doesn't know how to finish *The Apology* under the weight of his own specious reasoning. It's possible that Pascal's tendency toward incompletion isn't as involuntary as I would have thought at first, as the *pascal*, a noun that represents a unit of pressure in physics, is better than the adjective attached to the lamb of God, anyway this Pascal is for everyone, favoring the transportation of individuals without, theoretically, considering rank (*omnibus* means everyone's bus, from the king to the poor miller's youngster), but the royal privilege excludes "soldiers, pages, lackeys, and other liveries or individuals in uniform, as well as unskilled workers and laborers," an exclusion of rights already established by the five-shilling fare. It's clearly stipulated in the *Letters Patent* that each passenger should pay for a seat at a fixed price, five shillings and never more, whether the vehicle be full or almost empty. Hence on the 21st of March, 1662, Madame Périer, Blaise Pascal's sister, shares the good news about the success of the coaches with Arnauld de Pomponne: "The thing hath beheld so great a success, that as early as the first morning we witnessed full coaches and even the presence of some ladies [...] ."

Elsewhere, the noun *carabas* is documented (Littré, along with Trésor de la Langue Française and Larousse, still recognize the spelling "carrabat") as a possible distortion of "char-à-banc," an open-topped public transportation wagon with bench seats, like the wagon that was used during the Age of Enlightenment to load twenty people in Paris and bring them on a four-and-a-half-hour-long trip to Versailles.

In turn, the Parisian Regional Transportation Authority (RATP) circulated an advertising leaflet in 1986 to promote its late-night buses, using the slogan, "After midnight, don't go home in a pumpkin anymore." Anyway, hop on!

Pshshshsh . . .

For Basile, "on time" always means early. He's always itching to know what time it is. Managing time is his purpose in life. That schedule to follow. Those kilometers to cover while staying focused on the minutes: to not be late, or too early. Ever since his first days in the driver's seat, he has always seen the steering wheel as a clock: "Hold the steering wheel with your hands at a quarter past nine or at 10:10." His arms have become the hour and the minute hand.

On the dashboard, no bobble-head dolls slide around, no pin-up or dried flower hangs from the rearview mirror, no family photo, no Saint Christopher medallion or any other miraculous coin. I see Basile as a sober sentimentalist who keeps his affections secret and who has never felt hatred.

The world is at his feet and unfurls beneath them. Floating, Basile slurps up the ribbon of the road. In the rearview mirror, he gazes at the road gone by in the same way you might contemplate faraway stars on a clear night: the image seen is ancient. It goes by too quickly, or not quickly enough. The good-bye to his wife standing in their little yard where she cares for the roses—too quickly. Not quickly enough—the newly plowed plains where nothing grows yet, at least to the naked eye. If he wanted to, he could, on demand, relive the best days of his life. It wouldn't take long to add them up.

Basile isn't an unhappy man. He's conscious of his fragility. To force the contrast of an exception, like tossing a stone in calm water to make things out more clearly, I presume that he carries an old wound, a small preoccupation that pulls at him like a void—might it be taking him over?—a wound he himself has patiently invented a method for coping with.

The engine warms up. The bus is ready. Basile backs it slowly out of the garage. He makes his way across the sleeping town, squeezing through the narrow streets. Oh, the mill is quiet! In a series of delicate maneuvers and turns whose geometry he knows by heart, he brushes by heavy stone façades and shutters that are still closed. Here and there, a kitchen timidly chooses the right moment to light up.

Everything is dark, cold, and hungry.

Basile parks his bus at the little square. The cafe is lit up. Three regulars have already started their day, sitting like pillars, hunched over with their elbows glued to the bar.

Pshhhh . . .

While Basile goes in to sip a large black coffee and eat a slice of toast, the bus's engine continues to warm up. The passenger door is left open for air circulation, in the front, on the right. Anyone could hop on.

And so we hopped on, aspiring to act as a witness, wanting to sit back and observe. We, being of royal blood, but disguised as a commoner again, as a clandestine passenger of the bus, have decided to get on for amusement, with the purpose of experiencing, without an intermediary, those we represent, calmly and harmlessly observing, giving in to the archetype of the story-book prince who doesn't know how to rule and so takes to the streets, the souk, the marketplace, dressed like one of his subjects. The royal we, meaning I, and may it also mean you, bus specter, I hollowed out from a true I, if it's true that in the tutelary shadow of Julio Cortázar's *Cosmoroute* and in Gu Menda (Lino Ventura)'s trip down to Marseille in *Le Deuxième Souffle* [The

Second Breath] by Jean-Pierre Melville,[4] *I* linked Embrun and Varengeville-sur-Mer alone by bus in nine days, from the 11th to the 19th of November, 1988, of course it was an intentional stroll, but I never succumbed to the clichéd role of the wanderer, approximately 1200 kilometers, only the points of departure and arrival were explicitly set, the stops in between being determined by the caprices of exhaust pipes, but nevertheless subject to my rule of no trains, no taxis, no hitchhiking, and no car rentals: Gap, Grenoble, Valence, Le Chambon-sur-Lignon, Le Puy-en-Velay, La Chaise-Dieu, Arlanc, Vichy, Monluçon, Châteauroux, Blois, Orléans, Dreux to Saint-André-de-l'Eure was an exception (twenty-five km on foot), Évreux, Rouen, Saint-Valery-en-Caux, Varengeville-sur-Mer, all for a total of 685.20 francs in bus fares, room and board, some other standard knickknacks, and nothing really special to say about it all. It was a trip without surprises. Nothing happened. There was nothing to do except stick to the rule and try to observe, which made the trip an ordinary one. What disappointment, then, must be hiding behind the title, *My Beautiful Bus*! Unless a thousand things already seen and considered silently fuse with the storeroom of accumulated scenes separate from the trip. For the organized trip doesn't rule out the unexpected. Instead it reaps the false unexpected, the exotic unexpected, the sort that

---

[4]Gu travels from Paris down to Marseille by bus to remain inconspicuous since he's on the run.

Autonauts of the Cosmoroute: A Timeless Voyage from Paris to Marseilles, by Carol Dunlop and Julio Cortázar, Gallimard, Paris, 1993. The travelers' rule was to link Paris and Marseille, "stopping at all 65 parking lots along the highway at the rate of two per day."

you find in twenty different guidebooks whose same twenty lines compete to predict the unexpected, including the level of surprise and admiration that's required of you, if you are worthy. The organized trip shifts perspective only slightly. Which isn't to say, however, that I will resign myself to merely describing this shift.

We, I, who am certainly Carabas deep down, Carabas lured by his homonym noun, this simple peasant Carabas having become a fat and languid king—happiness isn't as beautiful as the pursuit of happiness—adorned with all the ridiculousness that the proverbial meaning of the largely obsolete noun conjures: a *carabas* is a fake nobleman, a pretentious arriviste who quickly becomes infatuated with his title . . . Carabas, having renounced his duties, set on questioning, incognito, the lowly parts of the world to find out what's really been learned, what the people of his kingdom are thinking. Wouldn't it be something if it just so happened that, plain and simple, my subjects didn't give a damn about the Koran, compared to turning forty? Or perhaps I can observe how they nourish themselves with pure wine and love, and how they cope with their romantic troubles. Like my own potential problem, for example, the one that would arise if the queen were to find out that I'm clearly a peasant, and, feeling betrayed, throw me out.

How does the common world live through its troubles? How do others go about loving, and how do they handle love when it trembles at its foundations? Can I learn something from their example?

Our invisibility in the bus, a gap, the hollow *I* like a fly whose veins have been sucked dry by a garden spider and who, in a nightmare, becomes a vampire, a Dracula, which means that it can now take its turn drinking the blood of others, this kind of fictional character (especially when he's the narrator), is zombie-like. If it looks like blood is flowing through his veins, it's really just water dyed red. While watching the Disney Channel yesterday, I giddily jotted down an implicit reflection on this *I* character: in the Walt Disney version of Dickens's *A Christmas Carol*, Scrooge McDuck is Scrooge, Donald is the nephew, and Mickey is Bob Cratchit. But Mickey also plays Paul Dukas's *Sorcerer's Apprentice*, based on Goethe . . . I immediately found myself imagining Mickey Mouse as Puss in Boots, a beautiful contradiction that might pass unnoticed given the strange role that this sort of character plays. (It would be the same sort of alchemy if Charlot—not his American persona, Chaplin—were to play Jesus, for example.) He isn't exactly an actor playing a character, because this actor is already a character, but more precisely a multidimensional character, who's nevertheless still contained by the dimensions of his sort, loosely employed, readily hosting an array of characters in his mold. There's something similar about my narrator, *I*. He has to be a stereotype, a jack-of-all-trades, capable of seeing everything and being in every situation, without ever failing to keep a distance, the least burdened as possible, from the author's idiosyncrasies, refusing to give in to them or at least resisting them as much as possible. But this can't be done. An author doesn't know how to hide himself behind his characters. Instead he shows himself naked through them, and rhymes with them all.

And so I've embarked. Which seat should I pick? The one that's best for stretching my legs or the one best suited for propping my knees up at eye level against the back of the seat in front of me? The one that offers the best view of the landscape or the passengers or the driver? A window seat halfway back on the left? Up front on the right for the conversation? In the very back with the middle-schoolers? Actually, I have the luxury of changing seats as I wish, without being noticed or suspected. So, it's decided: I will read, as if this were a book, everything that would ordinarily be kept secret. And I will try, naïvely, to learn some lessons from it all.

As soon as you get on the bus, you're greeted with three rules clearly posted on a written sign: no smoking, no talking to the driver, and no exiting the bus while in motion. Hello, good listener and good reader!

The second rule is rendered unnecessary by the bus driver's own attitude. He certainly must hear what his customers say to him: a hello, a good-bye, an expressed curiosity, and the destination, for which he must calculate the correct amount due. Basile hands over the right tickets, hands back the change, gives a "thanks" with a nod of his head, and moves on to the next customer, but he never answers questions.

"Where are we headed?"

It's written on the sign on the front of the bus.

"Where are we coming from?"

Is it possible to know where one is coming from, at a point somewhere between the chicken and the egg?

"Where are we?"

You should know just as well I do, you who have consciously boarded the bus at this precise location.

Basile remains silent. Everyone knows this. But although he's silent, he isn't completely mute. He speaks with his habits. Basile doesn't sing, doesn't yell at the road or his vehicle, other drivers, or the cops. He doesn't disseminate the usual banalities.

He doesn't hold long conversations about the unpredictability of our era. Basile is far away.

Pshhhh.

It's departure time. Mechanically, Basile has already checked behind him to see if the little steel hammer is in its place, the one used to break the windows in an emergency. Everything is in order. Someone has boarded alone, an ordinary, older woman who's too warmly dressed for the trip, headed out to kill a few hours in the next village along the bus route. She will take her time making her way back.

The bus will remain mostly empty during the first part of the trip, which is still very mountainous: short distances connecting small villages, and short stops for a single person here and there. To win over his passengers, a driver must know when to let one of them off between two official stops, or even when to let one on at the end of a dirt trail. He also has to agree to deliver packages, boxes, foodstuffs, and newspapers. Sometimes, in spite of all of his efforts and his many years of experience, Basile arrives at a village stop early. He has to wait for the exact departure time, with the bus door open, scanning the empty landscape for a sign of a passenger, a regular, rushing to catch the bus. Most of the time, no one comes. Or someone will be waiting half a kilometer away to flag him down.

We're still winding through the narrow part of the route, heading down from the pass, the part of the journey that never seems to end. The undergrowth is moist here. Rocks tumble from the steep slopes and roll onto the road. The slope on the shady side is mushroom-laden. With a bit of luck you might spot a squirrel scurrying about, darting incessantly in all directions, and, perhaps once every ten years, a bold pair of mountain goats.

It's the icy part of the route when winter insists on it, the part where you feel sick in the morning on an empty stomach, and the part where the sun makes glorious halos two months out of the year at a precise time of the day, piercing through the fog and the trembling leaves.

It's autumn today. Summer has been left behind in the rearview mirror. At high elevations, yellow needles fall, dying, from larches. The chestnut trees still hold on to half of their leaves. Further down, the oak trees will cling to their browned and wilted leaves until springtime.

Most of the time, passengers hardly look at one another. But look here, two are saying hi . . . I move closer and hear them whispering about their driver:

"He isn't talking any more than last time."

"Or any of the times before."

"Seeing how long this has gone on, I'm of the opinion that he won't ever speak again."

Which seems to suggest that he's talked in the past.

"A hopeless case."

As we get closer to the midpoint between the two small towns, Châtillon and the stop at La Chapelle-something-or-other, we begin to enter a zone of heightened magnetization. It feels as if everything that lives and feels, out of habit or by impulse, everything that admires or desires, is moving toward the town ahead. The effect of this phenomenon is a considerable increase in bus passengers.

In the courtyard of a saw-mill, a fire burns incessantly, fueled by wood chips and sawdust. Even the smoke flows in the same direction as my beautiful bus. The cry of the biting saw is earsplitting.

Basile turns on the radio to listen to the daily news. What's on today? Reports follow each other like days, and look a lot like one another: the famous are ill prepared for their inevitable obscurity; foreign trade is reviving; the weather is peremptory. There's a death toll; Basile hears the total and turns it off.

School is about to start and it's time to pick up all the classroom-bound-kids along the road to La Chapelle. It's conceivable that there's a big middle school there, since the stops are taking longer and the columns of twelve-to-fifteen-year olds are getting longer. The time must be taken to slide a few big bags into the luggage compartment. The school kids open and close the compartment door on their own. They board in bunches. There's the cocky kid, armed with a sole flap folder decorated with a garish sticker expressing his disdain for bulky schoolbags. There are those who rush toward the very back, the loudmouth boys with their little tiffs about who's on top. A girl has the right (or the cheek) to join them. She has entrusted her small backpack to her friend who has stayed up front, who isn't as pretty, and therefore doesn't have the same privileges . . . she resigns herself to isolation, but not without the pride of becoming, after the incident, a trustworthy confidante.

Basile daydreams about his daughter, their daughter, who drifted away from their world, moving further and further away day by day. This was necessary for her to be able to grow up, receive her high school diploma, and leave for Paris to study business. Everyone wants to study business these days. He broods over the vague fear that they may never become close again. An autumn feeling . . . like spring will never be seen again, out on the horizon, through the windshield. In his bus, Basile passes the house that he built fifteen years before, very slowly, brick by brick, he even got his own hands dirty in order to reduce the cost of the enormous project, completing all of the finishing touches on his own. How time flies! Not a leaf is left on the tree. He honks his horn, a greeting to the smoke drifting from the chimney, signaling that the central heating has turned on. He's well aware that there's no one inside the house and that the electronic salvation must have been triggered by the drop in temperature. The rose bushes that he has dressed with straw are ready for the tough season. The boxwoods sometimes freeze over. It snows on the gnomes. In the rearview mirror, once it has been passed by, the house is newer, the trees aren't as tall, the renderings are radiant; everything appears like it was not so long ago.

Basile isn't the kind of driver who goes out of his way to entertain the middle-schoolers. No zigzags through detours. No radio liberating its sound waves. Sometimes, during easy-listening hour, he's willing to understand the silence from a little girl passenger patiently standing beside him as a question, and answers yes by turning the radio on at a very low volume, as if with his own voice he were whispering a song in her ear.

More and more adolescents get on. After a few more stops, there won't be enough seats for everyone. Some will have to stand in the aisle, keeping their balance by holding on to the handrails. My beautiful bus shakes its passengers when it rolls over a speed bump, known to some as a sleeping policeman. Fog begins to film the windows on the inside due to the combined effects of breathing, conversation, and laughter.

At a village stop, before the recent rush of passengers got on, a young woman boarded the bus through the side door. She didn't buy a ticket. She didn't show a bus pass. She waved to Basile from a distance, communicating some kind of understanding between them. Some middle-schoolers, for the most part girls, say a shy hello to her, but keep their distance. She places a leather briefcase on the seat next to her. She will have to hold it in her lap soon. I'm immediately drawn to this passenger: she's beautiful without being too beautiful, small and of an indefinite age; she's smiling and curious about these people around her who are so easily surprised by nothing, and ask questions about this nothing until they find their special secret, always lying in wait for a slice of conversational pleasure. They will always find at least some pleasure. I have never seen her before; she reminds me of someone. I recognize her right away, with the strength of a resonating echo that I have trouble pinpointing. She has one hand that I believe I know, while the other is completely foreign to me; one eye has already seduced me, while the other can hardly see me. She stirs up feelings of pain and reminds me of my troubles. She is reading a book and a newspaper, alternately. The newspaper is regional. The book is thick. She holds back a yawn.

Since she got on, Basile can't stop looking in all of the rearview mirrors at hand, and, to that end, he even adjusts the left side-view mirror. She's the one he's looking at, no, observing, no, the one he's *staring* at, and the one he sees change shape and get larger, but only slightly.

At one point, she smiles at him and widens her eyes, as if to say "watch the road!" or "be careful!" or even "patience!" Then she lets her gaze drift away into the expanse of scenery flying by.

The bus on the road follows a fierce flowing river. The water is grayish, a sign of violent rains upstream. Random pickets hold back grass, sentences, twigs, shredded bits of plastic, giant masses of hair, everything that the current carts along, living molecules that compose and consume stories. Public dumping is a common occurrence. The waste unabashedly finds its way down to the riverbank.

Once the road reaches a particular hamlet, Basile stops, and pshshshsh. He waits with the door open. Is someone there? No, but something is. A pot with a cover held in place by a knotted dishtowel has been delivered right to the door by a limping old man. The man doesn't even announce what's in the pot. It contains mushrooms, oyster mushrooms. He only says "thank you," in a tone that implies more, that says that everything is happening as expected, a simultaneous "hello," "good-bye," and "it's understood . . ." and "I know everything about you that I need to know." Basile doesn't say anything. He knows to whom he should pass along this seasonal commodity: to the best restaurant in La Chapelle, which has the ironic, rhyming name of *La Gamelle*, the Lunchbox.

The bus is packed, but it's still a while before the empty seat next to the woman reading the book and the newspaper is filled by a young girl who is more daring than the others. Do they know each other?

"So, Nathalie . . . how have you been?"

"You remember me!"

"Of course! So, how are you? You're in eighth grade, right?"

"Ninth grade, ma'am."

"Already . . ."

"Yep. Actually, I have a homework assignment on Baudelaire . . . I wanted to ask you . . . Am I on the right track to suggest that his prose poems . . . um, well, that they were more modern than his *Flowers of Evil*?"

"Modern . . . Well in any case it's . . . Does he say that? Well, I don't know . . . I can't remember."

The woman reading the book refrains from saying: "I teach fifth grade, you know." Deep down she's thinking that she may never have really known the answer to the girl's question, and it makes her sad because it was nevertheless within her reach to know. She only has about two minutes to confirm the young girl's brand-new impression that she knows a little something about literature. She settles with encouraging her, hardly daring to dream about the big city Baudelaire envisioned, his conformity to an elastic style of prose, while through the window she admires the precision of the fields of plowed rows, the meticulous planting of young crops and vineyards, which are like lines of verse on a page. She lets out a sigh:

"I'll have to read it again ..."

And I bet she will.

Rush hour is over. The middle school and the high school are on the outskirts of La Chapelle. The youngsters have exited the bus, slowly and wearily, carrying with them a vague anxiety hidden under too much nonchalance. The closed space of the schoolyard—which in a sense belongs to them, after all—reassures them. It opens up its doors to them daily, with no exceptions.

Against the flow of the emptying bus, a fat woman gets on. She seems like the type who's just looking for something to complain about. She's only going as far as downtown and regretfully takes out a few francs, as if she were being forced to give away precious stones. It's expensive. To make sure that she gets her money's worth, she takes up two whole seats with her big bags. She sits down in the same row as the woman reading the book, but across the aisle. She wants to chat. To get the conversation going, she talks about the driver, which apparently isn't the best method.

"Out of all the company's employees, I like him the best. A very gentle man . . ."

And she smiles with a look of understanding. The fat woman waits for a response to her eloquent words, which won't come.

"And the most punctual. I'm telling you . . . It's been more than ten years that I've been riding this line at least once a week, you know."

The two women size each other up. Apparently the one who boarded most recently doesn't like the other one's small smile. It irritates her. It makes her realize how vain her words are. She's the type of woman who leans in close to whisper gossip but deliberately raises her voice to make herself heard anyway.

"Is he doing alright these days?"

"Oh, I don't watch over him."

"Well, I guess you're right not to."

"I don't know if I'm right. But that's the way it is."

"You're lucky!"

"Lucky . . ."

In the rearview mirror, Basile watches her answer. Does he know how to read lips?

He pulls the bus into its temporary terminus. It will make a fifteen-minute stop here. The fat woman exits the bus, grumbling. She has a hard time making it through the aisle smoothly with all of her bags, and no one helps her. That's always the way things go nowadays. The world is becoming wild again. She makes sure to say good-bye to the driver, but not to the woman passenger with the book.

Apart from her and myself, there's no one left on the bus. Basile comes over to her and tells her something, without speaking, something tender I believe. I can tell by the way he approaches delicately and cautiously. Pretty soon it becomes obvious that she's the person, the Odile and the wife, for whom he has decided to reserve the surprises of an inaudible language, a language spoken by only one person in the whole world: him, but understood by another person, and one person only: her. Keep in mind that if I want to remain faithful to the role that I have set for myself, at this point I will have to learn how to translate it.

And so together they whisper to each other, in their way. They tenderly hold one another's hand. It's break time for both of them. Odile smiles, which is paradoxically what betrays her faint sadness. Perhaps she wants to get back to her reading, but she surrenders to the duty of being present and paying attention. She says:

"If I have the energy later, I'm going to grade some of my students' notebooks."

The tone in her voice hints that she's somewhat dreading the chore, but that she's confident nonetheless. She knows that once she's gotten started, she will find herself completely immersed in the task, and will be ready to dote over a good assignment or congratulate herself for some evidence of progress.

"I don't have class today. If it's all right with you, I'll ride along your route with you. And I'll get off at La Ferté to see my mom."

He has a fatalistic expression on his face. He's surprised, from what I can tell, that she can write without difficulty in my beautiful bus.

"It's not exactly writing . . ."

But what about reading? It makes so many passengers nauseous. They say so themselves.

"Not me."

Would you read on top of a volcano?

"Why not?"

During an air raid?

"Even on Charon's boat, the boat that brings the dead to the other side of the river."

A rotten line of work.

"He'll make all of us get on the boat someday."

Not you.

"Yes, even me."

No.

Time . . . It's about time to leave again, time for the most distant collusions, using the rearview mirror or collective memories as the intermediary, amid the usual peacefulness of a trip without surprises, if all goes according to plan.

Pshhhh.

Basile turns the key to the ignition and puts the engine in gear. The motor hums, as it's supposed to. The turn signal blinks. The bus has the right of way as it leaves its stop. In a flash, Basile thinks about his back, the compressed vertebrae, which is a common condition in his profession. Others have it worse than he does. He thinks about the required solidarity between time and space, the Siamese twins of his toil. He awaits the sight of the mansion with a bare triangular pediment that he has watched crumble to ruins over the past twenty years, little by little, in the same spot. To keep his fear at bay, he inevitably muses on his two-part obsession, each part undoing the other: the first one involves him crushing a child under the wheels of the bus, a child that turns out to be his own daughter; second, he thinks about the punishment he would have liked to wish upon himself to prevent the first: a truck ahead of him carries a heap of scrap metal. A scrap severs the strap holding it in place, takes flight as the truck passes over a bump too quickly, passes through the windshield of my beautiful bus, and decapitates Basile the driver—a negative consequence of the fact that the new roads permit higher speed limits by bypassing the center of large towns. Fortunately, the bus, for its part, still has to pass through towns, regularly exit the national highway, slow down, and snake through the old road that all of the traffic was once forced to squeeze through. The bus has to wind its way to its stops at the plazas lined with plane trees, and be received ceremoniously as the vehicle of saving grace that opens up all of the Republic's enclaves to the rest of the world.

Odile has gone back to reading her book. Tilting my head a little, I make out its cover. It turns out to be a thick book by Doris Lessing, *The Golden Notebook*, which she is already a third of the way through. She fans herself with her bookmark, a postcard of the quays along the Seine in Paris lined with overhanging trees in bloom. Odile hasn't taken out her stack of notebooks.

I clear my throat and sit up straight to get her attention and to start my investigation with full force.

What are you capable of?

Will you tell me about something that happened to you in the past, something mysterious that you've never quite been able to figure out? Something that's very important, even fundamental, to your present life?

Will I have to ask you a few questions to get you started? Maybe a general, catch-all question?

Odile has lifted her eyes from her book to let them dart off into the distance. Yes, I'll have to ask her. She tries to avoid letting the rearview mirror into her field of vision, and manages this by perching her gaze on the far-off branches that drip with dew, on a tree with a missing limb, cut off one day to make way for a power line. She tenderly leans her cheek against the headrest and answers:

"Okay, what do you want to know?"

Oh, well it doesn't really matter what . . . as long as it's interesting.

"But, that's just it, I don't know a whole lot, I don't know everything . . ."

Your age. You're really young . . .

"Not that young, really. I'm forty-seven after all."

Well, the effects of aging obviously haven't taken hold of you.

She chuckles.

"Well, let's get on with it!"

Basile . . . Does he really not say one word? He hasn't spoken since . . .

"Since a particular trip."

Never?

"Never."

Even to you?

"He talks to me, in his own way."

Tell me what happened.

"I don't know exactly."

Tell me what you do know.

"Well, why not, after all?"

Odile has kicked off her ankle boots. Angling her position a little, she rests her little feet upon the seat. Her legs are clothed in plain white socks. She's wearing green, thick-ribbed corduroys.

Above those, a white linen sweater pinned with an antique broach, a cameo. She tries to make herself comfortable, testing several positions. She pulls down the armrest and puts her legs over it, situating it between the thigh and the calf. A foot slides underneath the other foot to keep warm. She closes her eyes, without sleeping: gentleness, power, strength, and nonchalance. Puss in Boots is obviously a female. It's undeniable if we take a look at Constantin le Fortuné (the name of the youngest heir)'s cat in Straparola's version of the tale, which Perrault read, and to which Pierre de Larivey even grants a feminine orderliness in his translation. In Larivey's translation: "The poor old woman, burdened by the years, and troubled with sickness, feeling death coming on, wished to expend *what little strength she had* left to write her will [. . .]" Perrault's version: "A miller left all of his possessions to the *three offspring he had*. [. . .]" In Straparola's version, the pussycat is the one who turns the brute into a well-groomed gentleman, in both literal senses of the word, when she bathes him in the river, like Clotilde, the Burgundy princess who baptized the Frankish king Clovis I.

. . . led him near the course of some river, where she made him strip naked, and afterwards dipped him three times in the water; then with her tongue, diligently licked him from head to toe, combed him with her claws, and carried on with this duty so meticulously that in less than three days she transformed him into a healthy strapping young lad.

Perrault's sacred pussycat, the muff who seduces any foolish rabbit into the sack, always leaving her sack open, tenderly satisfying herself with her catch before crushing it into a corpse with her boots! Puss in Boots is the quintessential feminine power that enables the masculine to succeed, to wear lace frills and ermine coats, just as she, Odile, I can sense it, limited her womanly ambitions one day in order to spare her companion, who she believed she had chosen, from a foreseeable chaos of angst: in other words, the old story of love getting confused with altruism. And some tellings of *Puss in Boots*, contrary to Perrault's version, agree on staging the ungratefulness of the new prince toward the architect of his success. Obviously he should have no right to know anything about her undergarments.

Odile tells her story.

"He had a fit of madness . . . a malfunction. It was during the very beginning. We had hardly known each other for a year. Basile was very handsome. I found him handsome."

He must have loved you madly.

"I don't know . . . More than anything he was . . . I guess you could say . . . surprised by me. That's it, surprised. He looked at me as if I were dressed in wrapping paper with ribbons tied around me. And with the kind of ribbons you can't cut right through, the kind that you need to spend your entire life carefully untying, while making sure to keep the wrapping paper folded neatly too. I had to push him, however little, to get him to declare his love for me."

Yes, faced with your beauty . . . he must not have believed his eyes.

"It wasn't really because of my beauty . . . What beauty are you talking about anyway? It was just the fact that I was a woman, which meant I was from another world. And so we tiptoed through our engagement, and marriage was like walking on thin ice. I, too, was a little naïve."

So you went away on a honeymoon . . .

"It wasn't exactly a honeymoon. We had already been married for six months, busy engaged in discovering one another. It was more of a . . . confirmation-moon. Before then, I had abruptly decided that my studies didn't interest me anymore. I had nevertheless gotten off to a good start. I was studying history. I could have pursued my interests much further . . . but I let go of them, managing to convince myself that it was a relief. Basile was happy. I was happy that he was happy. And therefore, so that it couldn't be said that I completely folded, I put the brakes on my ambitions: I decided that I would teach young children—as if they were any less engaging than adults! That's what I've been doing ever since, and I can't say that I don't enjoy it."

The trip . . . where did you go?

"To Paris. I was the one who picked Paris, where I hadn't been since I was ten. You know, we still make our children read pretty little stories about the countryside, like *Little House on the Prairie*, and sing sweet country songs like *Home on the Range*. But what more accurately defines the exotic for us provincials is the big city, which frightens and attracts us. My exotic, as it turned out, was immediately the biggest of cities. I had an aunt in Paris, who I liked a lot. I only knew her through correspondence: she regularly wrote to my parents who entrusted me with responding to her. As soon as I turned seven, every year as a birthday gift she would invite me to spend ten days at her place. Since she was assertive and she had some wealth they would inherit, my parents weren't able to completely say no to this proposal. They simply waited a year before deciding I was ready. If they'd only known . . .

"When I arrived for the first time at Austerlitz station, no one was there waiting for me, contrary to what was planned. After a long moment of anxiety and tears, I found myself in a taxi, taken in by a charming couple that had managed to get the details out of me about where I was supposed to be staying. My aunt lived on Rue Galand, in an apartment overlooking the garden of the Eglise Saint-Julien-le-Pauvre. She was a grand woman, seventy-five years old, terse, and a freethinker. To avoid being marginalized even further, she had hidden the consequences of a serious illness from my parents. It was immediately apparent to me how serious it was because she never went out, a secret that was enough to explain her absence at the station and which I would always keep a secret. She spent most of her time in her bedroom. I was never allowed to follow her in there or even take a peek. She welcomed me, expressed a sort of pride for my resourcefulness, and then she told my parents, who were worrying about me, on the phone, that the package had arrived without a hitch.

"As early as my very first stay, I knew that it was going to be wonderful. My aunt was very eccentric, and at her place I was left completely to my own devices. My discovery of the market at Maubert plaza was enough to keep me occupied. It was held there every other day, if my memory serves me right. I got up early in the morning, and because my aunt didn't emerge from her secret bedroom until eleven, I had learned how to make myself a solid breakfast. I would get dressed, put on my shoes, and go out alone with a bag and some money until lunch, which we never had before one in the afternoon and which lasted for two or three hours, and only after long and complicated preparations. My aunt would move around with the help of a walker that she called Firmin and would exhaust all of the muscular energy that she had at her disposal for the day. At the table, I reported to her what I had seen and bought for the meal.

"She would then explain to me what I hadn't understood about the visible world. During the days when the market was closed, I would tell her about the Maubert market and the plaza's shops in detail. I would describe the different stands. When she asked me to, I would draw a diagram on paper, a layout of how the sellers were arranged in rows, and a drawing of each stand and what it was displaying. If my memory wasn't faithful, she would encourage me to go back the following day to complete my depictions. The fish sellers interested her a lot. I would have to recite to her the names of every edible species and describe its shape and color with precision . . . was it a saltwater fish or a freshwater one, or both, eels! And which ocean and river was it native to . . . and octopuses, how do octopuses live, and crayfish, how can you distinguish between them and scampi? You will ask the fish seller, and yes, you will buy something from him for our dinner, because otherwise, I know him well, he won't tell you a thing. And make sure that he keeps the heads on, so that we can search for the otolith together, the fishes' internal ear. And make sure he doesn't empty them, because I want you to learn how to remove all of the guts without breaking the mass of soft roe on the inside. Then ask him if he wouldn't happen to have some glasswort, and if not than percebes, or goose barnacles, those little crustaceans like the ones you find in Galicia and the Madrilenian markets.

"As far as butchers, she insisted that I know how to find my way around the atlas of beef parts: 'So, what part of the cow does the hanger steak come from? No, not from the tail, silly, and are you sure that you didn't spot one at the tripe-seller? Alright then, tomorrow you will pick up a hanger steak, a tenderloin, a flank steak, and a skirt steak, and that way, tomorrow night, we will try all four of them to get an idea of how they're different. And listen here, when you're at the apple stand, don't pick out the prettiest-looking ones. Find the ones that look like they've experienced a little bit of life. Act disappointed if there isn't any fresh coriander, rabbit steaks, sorrel or tarragon, Chinese artichoke, and sow thistles. The fellow will end up finding you some. And if he doesn't, tell him he should consider changing his line of work.'

"I was careful not to blindly follow all of my aunt's advice, since she didn't hold little mistakes against me if I knew how to compensate for them by bringing her back something unexpected. At this rhythm, I learned a lot of things that my childhood in the countryside hadn't gratified me with.

"I also had to conquer my apprehension when, to crown our meals, I was charged with the mission of going down to the wine cellar to bring up a bottle of red from Morgon or Moulin-à-vent. My aunt, who hadn't been down there for ages, knew exactly where every one of her best bottles was stored, down to the vintage and the producer's name. When I came back from the cellar, she would caress my cheek as if I were reporting the ambient temperature and had the hydrometer reading printed on my skin. I came to appreciate wine and gave up my fruit cocktails. I came to appreciate cheese and gave up hard candies.

"And so I went to Paris for my eighth, ninth, and finally my tenth birthday. Each year, I looked forward to it. And I believe that my aunt, without really showing it, also looked forward to seeing me. What did she eat during the rest of the year when I wasn't there? The question never passed my lips.

"I became the little darling of the merchants, who were soon forced to gather their merchandise for the following day with the help of an encyclopedia, or if they weren't doing research they were running all over Paris to find a few rare products from their competitors. I must say, I was a pretty good customer because, even if I didn't buy much, I bought a little bit of everything, and sometimes I was followed during some of my exceptional shopping trips by housewives with whom I attempted to share my expertise. I learned world geography through exotic fruits (back then they were a lot harder to find than nowadays), those multicolored products from the ends of the earth, the mysteries of various imports.

"'Yes, my little lady,' the produce sellers at Saint-Sylvestre would tell me, 'it's summer in Brazil right now, but how do you expect me to bring mangoes up here all on my own?'

"I was at that age when you're flattered to be treated like an adult, but when your inner child has some alarming awakenings. Which is how it happened one morning. I was loitering in the storefront of a candy shop that until then my aunt's curriculum had omitted. The colorful candy was not vital for my development, according to her. To compliment me for being such a conversationalist and for being such an altogether charming little girl, the sales clerk gave me a cornet of sugared almonds. I ate them until I felt sick, and then I conceived the devious idea of putting my aunt's tenderness, which to me undoubtedly appeared a little obscured by all this erudition, to the test. I came home earlier than usual, sucked on my sugar coated almond until the sugar coating had dissolved, and I proceeded to carve the almond into the shape of a tooth with a little kitchen knife. In the spot where the root would have held it in place, I delicately placed a little smidgeon of red ink to represent blood. When my aunt came out of her room, I held out the tooth to her in the palm of my hand and asked her, with the sad expression of someone who needed to be consoled, if I didn't need to slip it under my pillow. My aunt was baffled, and perhaps a little disappointed by my rebellious act. She said nonchalantly, as if in passing, that I was too old, and was ready to move on to another subject, to an array of questions about waterfowl for example, or rabbit behavior, or boar's meat, or others on durians, mangosteens, pistachios, arbutus berries, or don't you remember who the first global producer of cloves was? Zanzibar! I won't tell you three times. And remind me what you know about pollination, herbs, the foliage of the forests, trees, shrubs, precious stones, and all of the metals hidden in the bottomless depths of the earth . . .

"She brought her nose closer to the tooth and realized, I think, that it was fake. She didn't say any more about it, but the daily lesson went on so long and was so full that I got the feeling that she wanted to stuff it with substance, as if I were going to have to leave the following day and never come back again.

"'Tomorrow,' she said at last, 'you will go to the market in la Cité. That's where the flower market is. Soon you will know what it means when people talk about the fragility of human things.'

"Night came. I had an awful nightmare. I remember it as if it were yesterday. I was at a social gathering, dressed in rags, in the receiving room of a very dark castle, which was plainly an avatar of the forbidden bedroom. All my teeth were missing. My aunt insisted that I dance with her. She was dressed as in the days of yore, wearing a long gown with panniers. She was twenty years old. But I didn't want to dance, using my ugliness and missing teeth as a pretext. She shrugged her shoulders and effortlessly took off in a waltz. It looked as if she were being led by an invisible knight, but a skilled one at that, the kind who waltzes effortlessly. She came to a halt in a fit of laughter, ready to hold me in her soft muslin arms. At that moment, she seemed to be listening to a secret, or rather a message, like the one a domestic servant might whisper in his mistress's ear, but of course no material individual was speaking to her. Her expression became sad, so that I began to cry. Shakily, she said, 'Why do you have those teeth made of sugar? You've sucked on them too much and they've disappeared. Why did you trick me? I thought I had niece who was better than that!'

"She started waltzing again, but in the opposite direction and reluctantly. And I realized that the dance was unscrewing her body at her waist, halving her like a Russian doll. She reappeared whole again, twenty years older, cruel, shriveled, and smaller, and said, 'You mean child, you've been so greedy, you've broken my heart. You have an awful life ahead of you, and people will hate you.'

"And the dance started up again, again spinning my aunt through a whirlwind of years, so that she looked sixty when the song was over, and she said, 'You betrayed me, Odile, and now you'll have to pay for it. How could you be such a thief when I love you and give up so much for you?'

"Then the waltz faded to a murmur, and out of the calmness my aunt reemerged as the pedagogue that I knew. Laughing, she said, 'Don't be afraid. I love you too much. I won't eat you. You remind me of your father the day he stole that hen in order to fly to the moon, grasping her by the legs as she took flight . . .'

"The last waltz was barely audible. My divided aunt rolled under the wardrobe and the bed: two tiny, colorless marbles.

"That morning, I got up as usual, although exhausted. My

aunt had died in the enclosed bedroom, which I didn't know until noon because for me the morning had been a flowery outing. I had come back from the market, completely thrilled with my exploit: an immense bouquet consisting of one hundred different flowers, all of whose names I had perfectly noted down on paper, one of each species, which I thought would be enough to receive forgiveness a hundred times over for my guile and childishness.

"There were a lot of people in the apartment. The medics gently explained her end to me. They had found her lying stretched out on her bed, having died peacefully, after calling them to let them know what might happen. Spread all around the room were piles of books, newspapers, and photographs of young half-naked dancers, many of whom were black. The neighbor said to me, 'Well then. Since you have all of those pretty flowers, go and place them on her poor legs, they will help her with the journey . . . Then you're going to come to our house. Your parents will be here tomorrow to pick you up.'

"There you have it . . . That's my Paris as a young girl . . . the Paris I haven't seen again for so many years."

So the only time you went back was with your husband . . .

"Yes, after having struggled a lot to convince him. I was determined to go back. I wanted to show Basile those banished places of my childhood. It was a considerable change of scenery for him. He had never set foot in the capital. We were going there together: Oh, but not for very long, a short four day-stay, and for the first time. It was also the last."

How can you be so sure that you won't go again?

"I just have a feeling . . ."

She remains quiet and reflective. I let a few silent seconds go by, enough time to ponder my creation, doubt my reminiscences, doubt her resemblance to anyone else, and especially to the one who I'm making an effort to forget. Had I been followed in my escapade? Had I been suspected? That feeling of déjà vu . . . What can you do with that impression of resemblance when you know that a child can resemble an old man, a man a woman, a dog his master, and that it isn't out of the question for a hag to resemble a beauty? Shared things bring two separate bodies together in order to better distinguish between them. Dam, a concrete noun, rhymes with damn!, the exclamation, but eucalyptus doesn't rhyme with eucalyptus.

Odile has stopped talking.

Should I get her going again? Yes, it's a must. Alright then, so . . . this stay in Paris? Where were you? What did your hotel look like? Was it in good repair?

Odile had reserved a room in a modest hotel not far from Eglise Saint-Paul. It was on the bank of the Seine that she wasn't familiar with, but still only a few blocks away from her old hunting grounds. Paris had changed. Or was it the both of them? Easter fell in March. It was a cold season. Basile had already been a driver for six years, a provincial driver, at ease in the countryside, far away from the large metropolitan areas. He was afraid of the big city where he couldn't find anything that he was used to seeing, and dominating, from the height of his bus.

"Yes, I clearly remember how he was intimidated by my ease in the big city, and of my natural sense of direction. And so he needed to find something to spoil my joy and make us leave. At least, that's what I inferred from his attitude. At first he was clumsy, nervous, and awkward, which ironically drew more attention to us. He would stand for minutes on end, petrified, staring up at the caryatids on the porticos of buildings. Then, he had his little bout with folly."

Tell me about it.

"The first evening, there we are sitting at a table in a Chinese restaurant, where I'm asking quite a few questions about the more unusual concoctions. I'm ecstatic; I'm happy to be there, to share my wonder with him, to make him touch my memories with his own hands. I want him to eat shark and wontons, to nibble on some ginger and taste kumquats, all of which fail to cheer him up.

"Once we've left, it takes us a long time to admit that we're finally ready for bed. In the deserted streets, the weather is humid and cold. We walk round and round, we twist and turn, hand in hand, using the Eglise Saint-Paul to center our circles. Every time we emerge onto the little church plaza, Basile appears to move away from it, reluctantly, as if repelled at the perimeter by a tenacious force. He discreetly watches the clock tower. Our first night descends upon Paris. It's a little late when we finally come back to our room. I can hardly stand up straight. We go to bed and fall asleep.

"At the beginning of the following day, Basile began to balk at the idea of walks in the city. If he had had it his way, he would have gladly stayed cloistered in the four walls of the hotel room. When he did agree to go out, only three or four streets among the ones nearby fully satisfied him, three or four streets and the Saint-Paul square, with its little Wallace fountain, three or four streets and the apse of the Eglise Saint-Paul, where you can more easily catch a clear view of the cupola towering above. He walked cautiously, as if ready to take on any danger, staring down everyone who crossed his path. He never agreed to take the bus. On the second evening, he asked me in a chilly and anxious tone that caught me off guard, 'What time can it really be between the first and the twelfth strikes of midnight?' It was a question just as logical as it was crazy and he insisted on elaborating a bit. 'At which one of the twelve strikes of midnight is it exactly midnight? Would you say . . . on the last? Maybe so . . . However, the clock that strikes doesn't differentiate. It's midnight when the first strike rings and it's midnight when the last strike rings . . .'"

I guess during that moment it really is a sort of no-man's-time.

"Yes, zero hour . . ."

A few questions resolved.

"Resolved? No, it's an opinion that he didn't agree with. Instead Basile believed that during this lapse of time, oh, I don't know . . . that particular miracles were made possible . . . Basile suddenly frightened me. I had the feeling that he was trying to push me away, but more out of idolatry than disinterest or lack of love."

An odd kind of love.

"Yes, you could say that . . . The third evening, he leaves our room alone, just before midnight, thinking that I'm asleep. I follow him in lockstep, without giving myself away. He anxiously heads toward the church. Having arrived at the plaza square, at the foot of a small stairway that leads up to the edifice, he hesitates for a moment, then with determination he dashes toward the nearest café. He goes inside, attempting to keep his eyes glued to the bell-tower clock. In the bar, he asks for the phone and for the door to be left open. He dials his number, listens with one ear and positions the other toward the sound that will come down from the clock tower. He sets some change down on the counter. Midnight strikes. Basile has the phone glued to his ear, but he isn't speaking to anyone on the other end. I immediately conclude that he's on the phone with the speaking clock. I spot a silhouette as it breaks away from behind the fountain where it was hiding and watch it float toward the square. Basile has seen it. He rushes out of the café and looks around for a few minutes on the steps of the church, just like someone who has lost the keys to his treasure chest or something even more precious. Basile returns to the hotel at full speed, making it impossible for me to get ahead of him. What now? I let a quarter of an hour go by before going back up with the excuse I was looking for, but which wasn't going to be of any use to me. He's in bed. He isn't sleeping. He reassures me. He hadn't even started worrying about what might have happened to me."

Did you ask him what he was looking for on the square?

"No."

Why? You should have . . .

"I don't know . . . I didn't want to ruin our trip by confessing to lowly espionage."

I understand that. But still, to start off with silence!

"The following day was our last. He had insisted that we go to the movie theater, which pleasantly surprised me, since he isn't much of an entertainment-seeker. I impudently cut the ticket line to spare him the wait. He seemed bothered. On the way out, I lose him in the crowd. He loses me, deliberately, in the crowd. I don't know what happened afterward. I don't know anything, other than he must have gone back to the area around Saint-Paul, and that perhaps he had a meeting with a shadow. I wanted to catch him by surprise there at midnight, but my watch had been set back an hour—by him, naturally—and so accurately that I arrived when the clock struck one in the morning, after having wandered and waited in two different cafes, one after the other. I don't know what happened. All I know is that Basile didn't come back to the hotel until the wee hours of the morning. He was as pale as ghost. Then a smile came over him, a pretentious smile, but his was always that way. He told me that he loved me, and loved only me, and that never in his life would he hide a thing from me, except the reason that would prevent him from ever speaking a word again. I guess you could say that he ... kept his word."

The end of Odile's story is clearly final. I respect it, even as I notice a look of worry in her eyes, one that has been with her since he stopped speaking. I wedge my raised knees against the seat in front of me, a good meditative position for a perplexed traveler. I abandon the inhabitants of the bus for a moment to float back into my bad memories once again. I think about my own Idol, the queen, my wife, who hasn't said a word to me for days. Everything brings me back to her. I believed that I took this abandonment as a relief. But it weighs on me already.

In my beautiful bus, hours go by, days, weeks. On the left, a cold plowed field, wheat grass, russet grain, the gold glint of thatched roofs and varied states of the vineyards, a bridge or terraces being built, a water tower that wasn't there the year before, political campaign posters. Plowed fields again, subdued wheat, their husks flattened to the ground by thunderstorms, the combine harvesters occupying the entire width of the road, and the round bales like jelly rolls, products of the advent of new machines invented to conserve straw and hay. The items on Basile's agenda: the uninhabited thatched roofs, a few larks, endless rows of structures belonging to a breeder of cooped and enclosed quails, four-furrow ploughs turning over their claws from one end of the field to the other.

Driving through the town that holds the county seat, Basile doesn't read the exchange rates that are nevertheless displayed on a panel of a bank's façade, the little flags of the principal financing nations in plain view. At a scheduled time, he listens to the radio to learn the bare essentials about the immense world. Hezbollah is getting some attention. Race riots in the suburbs of London. The death of a celebrity whose name he doesn't recognize. But there's nothing, there's never anything about the sweetness of dusk in Palmyra; nothing about the emerald ice blocks of Vatnajökull, the largest glacier in Iceland, when they fall into the sea; nothing about a meal of warm oysters over a wood fire between friends in Fouesnant . . . The latter things only matter when they go awry. His own world is never on the daily news bulletin, all of the beautiful things that Basile notices and that constitute an event in his routine, everything that moves and feels. A monstrous pile-up would be necessary, a historic flood, a mudslide, or a terrible, familial crime harming every branch of a tribe, a crime committed by his ruthless hand. Basile thinks about it, envisions all of these splinters of life between his eyes, and, at the very end of the road, the fleeting point that morphs at every moment. But he does nothing to make them a reality.

Basile isn't a vulture when it comes to driving and is rather inconspicuous on the road. He never flashes the headlights excessively, and only honks if there's a pressing need. Hardly, if ever, does he wave to his colleagues when he passes them on the road. He never takes part in the squabbles over right of way between farmers and truck drivers, ambulances, the rare taxi, the police, and tourists . . . Basile reaches his hand out and extends his index finger. He points to a heron taking flight from the riverbed. Odile has looked up from her book. Her eyes focus on the pointing finger in the rearview mirror, follow it to the heron, then return to the even lines printed on the paper.

The speed of my beautiful bus has slowed. It will soon be past noon. The travelers have become progressively scarcer. On the contrary, the traffic on the road has increased: everyone's on the way home for a meal. The watchful eye in the rearview mirror, for reasons other than carefulness, appears more rarely. Keep your eyes on the road, Basile, and be prepared for the worst, it's the time of day when people cross the road recklessly, kids running late and dogs without collars, the elderly propping themselves up on their canes to delay, however briefly, the inevitable fall.

Basile's stomach grumbles. He can no longer tell whether it's really hunger or instead the sight of these places, the same ones he sees every day at the same time, which induce a salivating reflex accompanied by a slight involuntary torpor. It's that time of day when he allows himself to have a mint candy. Everyone gets off at the next stop: La Ferté isn't much more than a large market town without any major fortifications, but every so often it attracts attention for its livestock fair. The bus has stopped for a lunch break. It will leave again after a brief forty-five minute stop.

In the bus, Basile will eat lunch alone: a Tupperware of mixed greens, a few slices of cold pot roast, a piece of goat cheese, and an apple. He will drink mineral water out of a paper cup, then coffee out of his thermos. Odile has gone to see her mother, a crabby woman who has never really accepted Basile. It's mutually understood that Basile never visits his mother-in-law.

For her daughter—she isn't having any herself—the old

woman will have sliced up some cold cuts . . . way too much for one person, and she will have arranged all of it nicely in a porcelain platter with a flower pattern now evanescent from wear, along with a bottle of red wine, lettuce, cheese, and finished with a plum pie. And yet, Odile hardly does justice to this abundance.

"I don't know what's wrong with me, I don't have much of an appetite . . ."

"Eat, Odile!"

"Yes, but I'm forcing myself."

"Would you have preferred something else?"

"No, that's not it . . . that's not it at all."

"Well, what is it then?"

"Oh, nothing."

As for me, sitting in my seat, hunger isn't in my nature today. Only curiosity, waiting, and I'm not quite sure what else.

Basile daydreams, while chewing the roast and the fresh bread that he just bought at his favorite bakery. He dreams about his Odile, who he never stops seeing in his mind, even when she's a hundred leagues away. Basile, unworthy of even knowing how to touch her, instead touches an item of her clothing left in her absence and the bus seat that still retains her warmth. Basile, who has always struggled with the materiality of love, comes and sits in the seat she has left. He lets himself be infiltrated by the last of her warmth, by her special radiance that paints the drab space anew, rearranging the layout and decor. He keeps the seat warm for her impending return. She will have no grounds to complain that it's always too cold in these buses, especially for the legs, nor that it's always too hot when the heat is blasting or on days when it's blistering hot outside. Basile sips some water. Cheese. Apple. He could easily take a nap.

Some customers start to linger around the bus, those who are getting ready to board. An old man is there simply out of curiosity, for digestion, and a bit of daydreaming tinged with bleakness: he won't be one of those who will leave and see the landscape fly by. The vast world? All it needs is a bus to bring it together. Elsewhere, in the bistro, the soon-to-be passengers settle their lunch bills. Basile gets off and heads to the counter for an espresso, which has an altogether different taste from the coffee in his thermos.

"Not a drop! You have to decide for yourself . . ." the road worker unfailingly declares to him, Basile, who doesn't have any particular reason to deprive himself of it.

Every day, Basile hears the "Not a drop!" of the road worker, a "Not a drop!" that is now as vital to him as his pulse or the metered hum of his engine, every day, except on two out of every three Sundays when he has work off, and a few other days along the wheeling seasons of the year.

Basile doesn't greet the occasion with sadness. Nor with haughtiness or smugness. Basile is elsewhere; his whole being attests to it. An elsewhere that is much more serene than anxious, from the point of view of any common observer. But he isn't the same in the eyes of the observer who has decided to make a character out of him, at all costs, so that he can get something out of this journey.

My beautiful bus has once again taken off on its assigned path. Odile has returned to her seat. A few regular passengers are heading toward Villefranche, the end of the line. They have an exact idea of how long the trip will take. They are ready to accept every minute of it without getting impatient. They would even welcome a benign accident that would delay their journey and make for a story they could offer to their little clan. They travel on the lookout.

Of those standing on the side of the road, Basile knows to a T who is waiting for the bus and who isn't. Among those waiting, he can tell at first glance exactly who plans to board and who has only come to see a traveler off at the stop. The traveler who's going to get on carries something in his posture, perhaps it's an almost infinitesimal anxiety, which the professional can perceive. World order, which, annoyingly, the Republic knew how to establish, is a bus present at a set point at a set time. Between one point and another, the route's duration is set. The infinitesimal anxiety comes as a result of imagining the fragility of this order. Will the bus be at the meeting spot? Does it want to go where the sign says it's going? Is the bus really public and for everyone? Does all of humanity know that everyone has equal rights? Furthermore, the travelers who are already present on the bus do everything within their power to insinuate this doubt into the consciousness of the newly arrived traveler, since every public place sparks within its user a reflex of privatization. The stares of those seated, those already settled in, those already-theres who were once strangers to this place and have by now developed their routines, their watchful eyes weigh on the new comer, declaring themselves at home, judging him, and sizing him up. Will he be able to assimilate? Will he be forgotten to the point that he doesn't exist? I observe the procession of those who get on . . . That long aisle to walk under the public gaze. There's the individual who starts a conversation with someone who has arrived beforehand by asking a superfluous question; there's an Arab who complies to being twice as attentive to the already-theres, who have had the right-of-way for generations; there's the guy who takes his personal freedom a little too far by leaving his big bag on the ground in the aisle with a hand resting on top, so that it has to be straddled; there's the young, tall, blond tourist, who has stowed his enormous backpack in the luggage compartment himself before getting on with his satchel, and who makes his way up the aisle with a firm stride as if wading through a rushing flood, finally sitting, without the slightest bit of hesitation, next to Odile, even though there are a lot of other free seats. He brings along all the excuses that come with being from some northern place, excuses that you can't do anything but accept because otherwise it would be obvious that you're afraid of him.

Odile looks at the tall robust fellow without quite knowing whether she should find his stature repulsive, or if instead she should immediately let her guard down and let herself be seduced. His soft facial features contradict the intensity of his profile. In the eyes of our judge, there's some extra skin that lacks bone structure or muscles. He takes over the armrest.

Odile is unpleasantly impressed.

Basile's rearview mirrors haven't yet begun their fine, precise work. Basile is lagging behind Odile's present. Basile is all slowness and caution. Basile isn't up to speed with the movement of things.

I move closer to the unexpected couple.

The speed of Odile's reading has slowed considerably. She thinks to herself that she should turn a page in her book to convince the unwelcome arrival that he's harmless and hasn't disturbed her reading, or to simply let him know that he doesn't have a chance. But the newcomer is the stronger. Right from the start, he crossed the usual line that separates two strangers from one another. Nothing can be done about it. He's interesting. In a voluminous gesture that impedes on Odile's space, he takes off his sweater and is left in a t-shirt, his arms bare to his biceps. Evidently, a body odor intrudes on Odile's intimate bubble, a smell that is neither displeasing nor pleasing, just a smell . . .

The young man, who doesn't really know what to do with his huge arms, stretches them out in front of him. His enormous hands have gripped the seat in front of him, as if he were going to break it to pieces. He sneezes, holding it in a little. He sneezes a second time, this time without reserve, letting his whole mass shake. From what Odile can tell, this is obviously done to disturb her. The hairs on his right arm are a few centimeters away from her, they're right there . . . The blond hairs stand on end like cornhusks at the end of the miniscule protrusions formed by goosebumps. Odile doesn't let her eyes drift up to his shoulder. This portion of the arm between the elbow and the wrist is enough. She could almost swear that she feels a warmth hone in on her, as though from a toaster, or an electric heater with red-hot coils, or a thick log in a fireplace when the smoldering side is turned outward. It's his body that has this thermal power. She could touch it. What's stopping her from brushing her palm against his arm with the most sensitive nerve endings in her fingers . . . ? The skin's fuzz only stands erect for a short moment, like when a peacock spreads its tail feathers, but only a modest tail. Or it's a line of trees arrayed along a crest, the soldiers of an army marching, leaning into the wind. Odile feels no impulse to photograph the phenomenon, but feels a desire to press her cheek against this meadow grass, or even her lips, at this precise moment when the raised hairs initiate their movement of refolding, which will lay them to rest again. This descent is extremely languorous. Odile shivers.

He speaks, and everything goes quiet, as if by a fatal spell. She's immediately hit by a wave of disappointment. She needs a little time, a few seconds, to regain a desire to listen.

"Hello, my name is Hans."

". . ."

"You didn't say *à vos souhaits* to me . . . That's how you say *Gesundheit* in French, isn't it? If you sneezed, I would have said *à vos souhaits*. I wouldn't have dared say *à vos amours*, but you can also say that, can't you? . . . And I would have wished, aloud, that among your wishes was one to listen to me, and I would have wished for your wishes to be mixed up with your loves, the ones that you haven't yet fully grasped. Let's face it, really, it would have been easier if you were the one who had sneezed rather than me. I would have wished you lots of love. If I were a girl and you were a man, you would have already been flirting with me for a while now. The reason why I don't flirt, if this is truly the case, is because women don't give me any respect for it. They feel like I'm betraying nature. What do you think?"

"Not a whole lot, but don't wait too long, in any case . . ."

"That doesn't matter . . . the important thing is to participate, and it really isn't a big deal if . . . Well, we can at least chat, can't we?"

"Where have you come from?"

"I'm from Weimar, well, the region of Weimar. I've traveled across Germany and I want to travel across France, and I want to travel across Spain, and the Strait of Gibraltar . . . after that, I'm not sure."

"Are you hitchhiking?"

"No, not hitching. I take the bus, sometimes the train, sometimes I walk. I've been counting buses. This one's my eighteenth. I keep a journal of profiles and encounters. I read a little bit. I left exactly ten days ago."

"You sure haven't been a slouch."

"I take the first bus that shows up and is heading in my approximate direction. I don't have a fixed itinerary. I'm not in a hurry. No one's waiting for me anymore. The chances of you and I meeting were really quite slim, you know?"

"So you're German? I thought that every German had an RV of his own!"

"Laugh all you want. My mother was French. When she was joyful, my father grew sad, and when he was sad for a long time, she would sing him gloomy tear-jerking songs, which would always end up making him laugh. After the war, she went into the striptease business and was in a cabaret show with him. She was so beautiful. It took her fifteen minutes to undress completely. My father was a magician. He raised chicks and doves. He taught them how to endure confinement in preparation for his best tricks. The day of my tenth birthday, I saw their show: my father began nearly completely naked on stage, wearing nothing but a G-string. That was how the burlesque began. He was skinny. My mother was sumptuous, wrapped in a fur coat and wearing a hat, long gloves, and black stockings. One at a time, she would take off a piece of clothing, a woman's piece of clothing, and my father would grab it, and presto!, change it into a man's piece of clothing and put it on: the fur coat became a shirt, the skirt slacks, the corsage a tie, the stockings socks, and the bra would change into a double breasted suit. Only the shoes remained shoes, losing their heels. When all my mother had left was her thin white silk panties that covered her *frifri* (you say "frifri" in French, don't you?), she would slip it off like a weightless piece of string, and the moment that she brought it up to her proud chest to throw it up into the air, my father accompanied her gesture by transforming the panties into a dove, which beat its wings out into the audience, holding a little laurel leaf in its beak. The show was called "Friedensnacktarsch," I'm not sure how to translate it . . . 'bare-ass for peace,' or something like that. My father had been an officer in the Wehrmacht."

"You're spouting nonsense."

"If that's what you want to believe . . ."

"After the war . . . you weren't even born yet!"

"When did it end, according to you? The 'postwar' period?"

"What about your mother? What happened to her?"

"She settled down, got older, and died. She had become a boring woman. She didn't fantasize anymore when she undressed in the evening. Do you like Mozart's *Requiem*?"

"Yes, of course . . . Do you always jump around from one subject to another like this?"

"I heard it last week, randomly, in Würzburg, where I stayed for the night in a church. A Requiem should never be sung if there isn't a coffin surrounded by an orchestra and choir. That is, an occupied coffin, of course."

Odile backs away slightly to get a better look at her conversation partner.

"You've got such a huge bag! What on earth can you be lugging around inside it?"

"If you want it, it's yours."

"What do you mean?"

"The bag . . ."

"I'm talking about the one that you stowed away in the luggage compartment. It's going to be freezing cold when you go to retrieve it."

Why am I talking to him about this, Odile wonders, as she proceeds with her technical explanation: "You know, it's freezing in a bus's luggage compartment in winter. Your clothes will be cold. The pages in your books will be cold . . ."

"Yes, I'm aware of that, and it's all for the better. My bag has to be kept cold, it's a question of life or death."

"What are you telling me?"

"Nothing yet, but I will. Will you hear me out?"

If you're polite to a traveler, you never know where you'll end up. A traveler is a transparency. He has no past that compromises you, and no future to get in your way. He's sometimes full of banal stories that become impressive if he knows how to deliver them right, playing a role in them himself.

"Why is it a question of life or death?"

"What?"

"You know, the cold in the luggage compartment. Why are you so desperately counting on it to be cold down below?"

"Because of my cadaver."

"Your . . . *what?*"

"Do you need me to repeat it?"

"I don't understand . . . your baggage?"

"Come on, you heard me right! . . . I didn't say 'baggage.' Did I say 'baggage'? Admit that you heard something else. Come on now, don't ignore it. Tell me the word you heard."

"'Cadaver.' You happy?"

"That's it. My name is Martin. Hans Martin. I use my mother's name."

Pshhhh.

Hans has just opened a can of fruit juice he took out of his satchel.

"You want some?"

"No, thanks."

"It's nonalcoholic apple juice, here."

"I said no."

Just smelling the sweetish odor is enough to make Odile's stomach turn.

"That's too bad. You would have seen how long a little pleasant taste could last."

He drinks.

"That's all right. I'm going to tell you how my beautiful cadaver ended up in my bag."

Odile shifts her position. While I decide to change seats again, she situates herself to listen better, as if she were embarking on a long journey. I covertly make it to one of the seats in front of them, gluing my invisible ear to the crack between the seats.

"It happened one evening last week. I was in Regensburg, in Bavaria. At my request, I had been dropped off on the side of the road by an unexpected bus that wasn't following a scheduled route. Or maybe I hadn't read the timetable and the list of stops carefully enough. Night had fallen, and the inhabitants of the suburb had taken refuge in their houses. It was that time of night when the scarce taverns fill up with customers drinking their umpteenth beer. I chose the place with the least amount of people. I went in and headed toward one of the massive wooden guest tables; it was rectangular and there was a menu standing on the tray between the condiments and a little national flag. I turned on a wall lamp behind me.

"The owner was taking orders and serving, light-colored blouse with baggy three-quarter-length sleeves, black cotton skirt, and red apron. At that point, my bag wasn't as heavy as it is today. I had set it down in a dark corner. She spotted it nonetheless, and gave it an envious look. At the time, I didn't think too much about it.

"At first, she was routine, hurried, and efficient with me. When I asked her if she could rent me a room for the night, she responded with a cold yes, it was possible, but not without having given me a thorough look-over, until she was convinced, as I mistakenly assumed, that my wallet was big enough.

"I took my sweet time eating my sausage and red cabbage. I was in the middle of finishing off my second beer when the owner came and sat at my table, on the shorter side of the L whose longer side I was taking up. She looked exhausted, but more exhausted than the tiredness induced by a full day of service. I made a polite remark to that effect.

"'It's true,' she said, 'I can't take it anymore . . . but I'm going to pull myself together. Where have you come from? And what brings you here?'

"'Oh, I'm from Weimar, I'm traveling across Germany, and I want to travel across France, and I'm going to . . .'

"She wasn't listening to me. She was looking at me with a strange expression while lightly arching her back to tighten the fabric of the apron against her chest. She was pretty well endowed in this respect and her face was tender. I was fighting fatigue and a kind of anxiety, weighed down by what she was looking to get off her mind. I was sure that it wouldn't be long before I inherited her secrets. But she got up to serve two more rounds to two guys sitting in the back, who were smoking their pipes in silence while staring at the foam patterns on the sides of their glasses.

"When she sat down next to me again, she had taken off her apron. Her face had taken on an altogether different outline. Maybe she had freshened it up with some cold running water from the tap. Maybe she had traced the lines of her eyes with black, which appeared soft and wet to me, the color of an oyster saturated with a flavor of salt and algae. She sat down in the same seat as before, placing two short tumblers and a bottle of schnapps in front of us. She said *prosit* to me, *santé*. I clinked my glass willingly, and the schnapps was good.

"She asked me the usual questions about my trip, to which I responded without elaborating too much. I asked her a few questions about her business. She told me that she was a widow.

"'Have you been one for long?' I asked.

"She paused for a moment, before responding with an incomplete answer:

"'No, well I'm not exactly a widow, almost a widow . . . or I mean, yes, I am a widow!'

"I was going to ask for more details when the two costumers informed her they were ready to pay. She got up to settle the bill, but they thought twice about it. I mean, they paid for the drinks they had already had, plus two glasses of schnapps, ours having given them a craving. Once served, they got back to meditating, slowly sipping on their drinks. Then the owner slipped away behind her counter and closed a door. I immediately started to miss her.

"When she came back, yet something else had changed in her. She had slipped out of her white blouse and slipped into a pretty green low V-neck sweater, like this here . . . just like the green of your pants, are they corduroy?"

"Hey, don't touch them!" said Odile. "Focus on your story."

"This time, she didn't sit down. She placed her hands flat on the table and leaned forward to speak to me. She was trying to smile, to provoke me. It was obvious that she was making an effort. It was impossible not to feast my eyes on the landscape that was being offered. The sweater generously exposed her chest and couldn't manage to cover both of her shoulders at once. Her breasts, inside there, held by the white cups of a bra that pressed them upwards: her breasts were imperious. That's the word that came to my lips. And to tell her that her breasts were imperious—which is what I did almost without thinking—was equivalent to swearing that I was at their command, that I didn't have my own will, that I no longer had parents, friends, freedom, nor a travel itinerary, until they'd gifted me with every last bit of their bounty.

"She left again, for the last time, to close the door behind the customers, who shot me a jealous look before going out into the cold night. She turned out the main lights of the room.

"There they are in front of me again. She leans over the table to turn off the wall lamp. The only remaining light comes in from the street. I can tell by the way she moves that she isn't wearing a bra anymore. Her breasts are free, smaller, longer, and heavier than in the previous scene. And there, I reach my hand out toward their warmth, my hand gliding easily under her sweater. Are you still listening?"

Odile has closed her eyes. Hearing the question, she doesn't reopen them. She simply agrees with a discreet nod: I'm listening . . . go on, continue . . . don't stop again!

"It was at that moment that the transaction started. She says, while not rejecting my hand under one of the globes, my thumb playing around with its tip, she says:

"'You're going to do me a little favor, aren't you? You're going to promise me . . .'

"'Well of course, I promise you. What is it?'

"'My husband . . .'

"'What about your husband . . . ?'

"I had forgotten what she had already told me about being a widow . . . I wasn't interested. I was eager to have her lay out the terms of the deal, so that I could finally slip my entire head under the sweater and take my tongue to one of her breasts, and then the other.

"'You must promise me that you will take him with you on your trip.'

"'Is that all? Sure, we'll see . . . is that all there is to it?'

"'That's all there is to it,' she replies.

"Yes, but would I even want to leave after this? I made a willful effort to anticipate the fulfilled state of mind I was going to find myself in after making love, trying to convince myself that to stay would be unbearable. I swore on my life I'd carry through with everything she asked, so that we could finally make love to one another, immediately, on the guest table. She was drinking the schnapps from the bottle and drew my mouth to hers to pass me the alcohol, sending it down my throat in little squirts. I'd never known a game like hers before."

Odile has placed her hands on the seat in front of her and her forehead on the back of the seat. She looks down at her feet on the floor of the bus. She feels her light breasts under her, as inflated as they can be, yet so small. She's suffering, and doesn't know why. An infinite fatigue submerges her, and sadness too.

71

Hans Martin continues:

"We slept like lead weights on that table, wound together, our sweat, our tears, and our sweet and sticky fluids drying as we lay there.

"She awoke first, well before daylight, to cover me with my shirt and make some hot chocolate. Not one more word between us. I was exhausted. I got dressed reluctantly, responding with a quick movement to every piece of clothing that she held out to me. Since I was cold, she generously gave me her sweater. When I was fully dressed, she said:

"'Follow me. I'm going to show him to you. I killed him yesterday morning. I strangled him. He's yours.'

"When I found myself in front of that huge black plastic bag, a garbage bag closed at the top with a long white string, I was only capable of one thought: that I had given my word and I only had one to uphold."

Hans Martin has stopped talking. He grants a moment's rest to his listeners, to Odile and me, allowing us enough time for mute realization. Our thoughts go to the luggage compartment at first, slipping into the preserving coolness of the trunk. What exactly is in that bag? If Hans Martin happened to get off the bus without taking his bag with him, taking advantage of a momentary rush of passengers, surely that would constitute a sign of premeditation. Basile would be in a position to turn him in to the police, who would hunt him down. But Basile has followed the vicissitudes of the narration only in a fragmentary way: even if he's able to read lips well, he is also obliged to watch the road, and maybe he's busy enough brooding over old jealousies ripe to flourish again.

But I spend a prolonged moment with my mouth agape as I listen to the young German, another Carabas of this fable, whose grief Odile, like Puss, wants so badly to assuage, Hans Martin, the transversal character of my expedition, the bus being our intersection point, the element of a "character rhyme," as Raymond Queneau said about Proust and his own *Witch Grass*, knowing that he might have found a hint about the rhyme concept from Pascal, whom we meet again; at this point we turn to Pascal's observations on the Bible, which he in no way considered literature (though I don't much care what pseudo-proof Pascal draws from the Bible to determine the validity of the Scriptures; it's just as easy to draw from them a conviction of their fictional character), in which he finds a genuine system of rhymes:

> *Jesus Christ typified by Joseph, the beloved of his father, sent by his father to see his brethren, etc., innocent, sold by his brethren for twenty pieces of silver, and thereby becoming their lord, their saviour, the saviour of strangers and the saviour of the world; which had not been but for their plot to destroy him, their sale and their rejection of him.*
>
> *In prison, Joseph innocent between two criminals; Jesus Christ on the cross between two thieves.*[5]

Which is why Mary's husband also answers to the name Joseph: Jesus is and is not the son of Joseph of Nazareth. He's only his son in so far as the patron saint of carpentry is a rhyme with the other Joseph . . . Joseph of Arimethea. And isn't it Judah

---

[5] Pascal, *Pensées,* Number 768, translated by W. F. Trotter.

who sells the first Joseph to the Ishmaelites for twenty pieces of silver,[6] Judah, a rhyme with Judas? Jonas, three days inside the whale and Jesus, three days in his tomb.[7] Jesus, who runs away at the age of twelve, and teaches the doctors (or the Goliaths).[8] That's not all. What's more is the astonishment I felt when I read *L'Invention de Jésus*, I, 3, by Bernard Dubourg (Gallimard, L'Infini, 1987), in which Dubourg finally explains the origin of the name Carabas via Frazer and Philo of Alexandria: Jesus and Carabas are the most magnificently rhyming pair of all, as Perrault clearly suggests in the baptism scene, for example. Like Hans Martin in the back of a cop car between two vagabonds, one of whom is me, taken into custody by the police, to whom I don't immediately reveal my identity, to whom I won't tell anything, and furthermore what would I tell them? And would they even believe me, for that matter? If all of the fiction in the Gospels is the product of that network of rhymes, then I'll have written our adventures in the same way, in such an order, the following one being the consequence of the one immediately preceding or following it. It's not a question of honoring my subject in this way, but of engendering it in a calligraphic pattern. Capable, yes, capable: for example, Hans Martin was capable of being called Dupont in an earlier version of *My Beautiful Bus*, and had been influenced by a material and spiritual car accident—like Pascal on the Neuilly bridge, the duke of Roannez's carriage led astray by mad horses, a hair's breadth away from falling into the Seine, the nearness of the abyss having had a profound effect on the

---

[6] Genesis, XXVII, 26.

[7] The Gospel according to Matthew, XII, 38-40.

[8] The Gospel according to Luke, II, 41-52.

philosopher—in that version Hans Martin falls for the first time, and the documentation of the story is sewn into the torn lining of his ski jacket:

"In fact, I left ten years ago, just after my accident. It was in June. I had borrowed my cousin's car to go for a dip in the river at one of the spots that I preferred for its seclusion and discreetness. When I came to the little bridge, cruising at the fastest speed that the worn-out Volkswagen would allow, something in the front drive train broke, and the steering wheel stopped working. I had to pray for the mercy of the metal guardrail that spanned the bridge. The car was compacted into an unexpected shape, but still didn't fall into the river. It hung, hidden between concrete and the trunk of a willow tree. My docile and malleable body couldn't resist the compression of the sheet metal, and ended up tightly enveloped by this makeshift sarcophagus. I was unscathed but unable to move. No one was around. For three days and three nights, I remained in the wreckage, hanging from the side of the bridge. It was likely that I would die without anyone coming to help, and I truly believed that I was going to die from hunger, thirst, waiting, and isolation. However, salvation came to me from the river down below: a couple of lovers came for a swim, wanting to take advantage of the dark night and an unfrequented spot to make love in the sweet open air, a stone's throw away from me. You aren't going to believe me, but in spite of how hurt and exhausted I was, I took advantage of my own situation to listen to the moans of their lovemaking (they were quite a noisy couple). My own arousal was proof to me that I was still alive, and I waited until the end of their climax to let out my first groan."

Odile: "You're spouting nonsense."

Han's performance and voice anchor me to this place. I won't get off of my beautiful bus before him. And perhaps I'll stay on after he leaves, to enjoy the consequences of his appearance.

"I've tried really hard . . ." continues Hans Martin, "I've tried so many times to pass it along to someone else along the way. That's the game, isn't it? One time, I nearly managed to pass it on to an old woman who no longer had a damn thing to fear, having lived through two wars and all their attendant misfortunes, deaths in the family, cripples and babies all rode in the same carriage among ruins that smelled like old dust, among the cries of 'Juda verrecke' (something like "die, (dirty) Jew"), the shame shamefully dwindling, Frau Herta really did want to take it off of my hands, but she died before I had the time to make the delivery, and so my bag remained in a baggage locker, on the other side of Ingolstadt from the place where she welcomed death after seventy-seven years spent in Berlin."

Odile has crossed her arms and leans back against the bus window. She puts as much distance as possible between herself and Hans.

"You don't want my cadaver, ma'am?"

"Not a chance."

"And yet, the more I look at you, the more I find you're intrigued by it."

"What makes you think that I don't already have skeletons in my own closet? Did you know that where I come from, no one was really opposed to the deportation of Jews. If I'd had a Jewish friend at school, for example, I would have agreed to never see her again . . . I would have kept my mouth shut."

"You weren't born yet."

"Yes I was, but I was in the cradle. Already old enough to love."

"But still . . ."

"And Negroes? Have you thought about Negroes? For a long time I blamed myself for the ebony bodies crammed into the ship holds . . . and then I came to a realization. We don't have a choice. They're terrible things to look right in the face if we persist in talking about them. I didn't say that they shouldn't be talked about. So the world works. Do you still believe something about it needs to be changed? We can't spend our lives in awe of it, but not believe in it!"

"The world? I agree. The time has come to take another look at it. So, will you take my cadaver?"

Odile is worn out. As if she's been walking for hours in the mountains: climbing up, descending, through harshness and tender weightlessness, awaiting the end without losing the trail. Hans's speech caught her during her meandering, and drained her of her energy. Odile is no longer Odile, now that all of her defenses have softened up, her watchful profile, and her outfit.

"Tell me . . ."

Odile goes quiet. Confused, she relives the unfolding of a situation that could have turned out better. All it would have taken was a stern look . . . but she knows that she wouldn't have preferred that, that even though her disgust disgusts her, it's stronger than the desire for the alternative, a disgust that she hates like a false friend and that she hesitates to recognize as her own. Come on now, everything will work itself out through chitchatting.

"You didn't ask her why she killed her husband?"

". . . before he killed her. As a preventative measure, I suppose."

"Is that what you think about love?"

". . . or because he had big ears . . . This may shock you, but I believe you can find a shrew in every woman."

"And in every male? Yes, what can you find in every male? You don't want to answer?"

But Odile's sudden vehemence, her capacity to change register, has no effect on Hans and his impassability.

"You're some sort of a juggler."

"So? My cadaver . . . will you take it from me?"

"Yes, I'll take it, but under one condition."

Odile's tone was disdainful.

"More conditions? In general, conditions hardly improve my chances of succeeding."

"Rest assured, it won't go very far, it's a condition that you won't be able to fulfill."

"Go on."

"Tell me what my husband was doing on the night of Easter twenty years ago in Paris, between approximately midnight and one in the morning."

"Nothing could be simpler . . ."

"Are you still so confident?"

"At least tell me a little bit about him . . ."

"What do you want to know?"

"What he looks like . . ."

Odile doesn't tell Hans that all he would have to do is look up toward the front of the bus, or shift his position slightly, and cast a fresh perspective on the driver and take away twenty years of silence and loyal service from him. Odile remains vague.

"He's kind of a pure soul . . . It happened one evening in Paris. Paris was a hostile place for him . . ."

Odile tells her story of Easter eve again, but differently this time, more disorderly, the events tumbling over one another: a

church, Paris, the absence, a secret garden with a fountain . . .
In this new version, she provides a supplementary clue that I
eagerly make note of: Basile spends his time examining the stone
closely, the old blackened stone of Eglise Saint-Paul. He scrapes
the caching off here and there with his knife. He says that they've
started removing all of this grime from the monuments and he's
happy about it. He circles around and around the fountain, one
of Richard Wallace's fountains, whose four nymphs hold up a
pointed dome.

"... and then he disappeared for an hour."

"Ah! He met up with a former ..."

"A former what?"

"One last escapade to remember her by ... It's quite common,
and sad. I can see her all the way from here. She must have been
a really large woman ..."

Odile bursts out laughing. Hans's hypothesis is stupid
enough to provoke tearful laughter, but he didn't want to
seriously consider the mystery that was put forward. He's only
thinking about one thing, which isn't even the good riddance
of his cadaver. He's thinking about Odile's petite body, probably
soft, and delicate too.

"Yes, a real fatty, the more I think about it ..."

"No, that's highly unlikely. You've lost the deal. Basile was a
virgin through and through. You're stuck with your cadaver!"

"I don't give a damn about my cadaver. I don't really insist
on parting with it. Someone has to carry it so that others can
go on loving each other in peace or squabbling in peace, teasing
each other in peace, covering their eyes, poking their eyes out in
peace, so that in peace others can go on starting up businesses
and making children and manufacturing goods and exchanging

them, continuing to vote for each other, and at times even assassinating each other in peace."

"That's foolish, you're going to end up getting caught."

"Yes, I'll be disposed of like a lowlife or a dung beetle, with a disrespectful kick of a boot. Someone will turn me in. I'm expecting that day to come. Maybe it'll be you . . ."

"I don't think so."

"Some spy or another on this bus . . ."

Hans takes a look around.

". . . but I don't give a damn about my cadaver. Come with me. Help me carry it as far as the desert, as far as the rice paddies, as far as the bush. It will be a beautiful adventure, a beautiful lovers' journey. You'll see . . ."

Hans takes her hand.

"What will I see? Memorable things? Uncountable things?"

"No, countable things, things that you aren't prepared for: most of the time, from front to back, the buses will be a solid frame with no openings or windows, just dirty and totally opaque window shades that protect the interior from water, dust, wind, and sun. The buses don't go very fast."

"Well . . . I'll get drunk off of rest, slowness, and silence!"

"Silence? In a civilization of honking horns and blasting speakers, one that values a spirituality of decibels? It's true that not every one of the hodgepodge of hours that make up a trip is remembered. In construction sites, women are the ones who clear out all of the rubble with those bins that they carry on their heads . . . You know, even though the misery and the crowd are to be expected, you still have to be prepared and fit in. Immediately given a rank, in your place right away, a fragment of the crowd, you don't have to think too much about it. On the contrary, your gaze is enraptured by the minute, unexpected details, as if they were so-called 'wild' animals."

"The smiles of the beautiful children that aren't yet damaged, for photographs."

"An ugly child crosses the street playing with a makeshift plastic-bag kite that fills with air. In Colombo, a truck full of Buddhas looks just like a clip-art symbol of a bus: six Buddhas sitting cross-legged on the truck bed, looking like old firefighters hollering with their hands cupped to make their voices carry further. A carefully tended lawn has tropical leaves in the tropics. Seen from an airplane, the communities of the Persian Gulf burst with light at night, whereas the lighting in restaurants in Madras is set so low that the menu can barely be read."

"I'll drink from fountains. I'll eat among the treetops. All I'll have to do is reach out my hand and lean over to pick a fruit."

"Suspicion of the water quality, the no-drinking rule that we ignore. The unloading of a truckload of bricks, thrown in stacks of five, they look like they're stuck together. Chinese restaurants without chopsticks. Mexicans without the shade of a sombrero. The only parts of the lower back and the side that the sari leaves naked, the parts of the shoulders and the back that the loincloth, a lamba-oana, or a paréo leaves naked. Scaffolding: logs roped together in Cairo, nailed boards with buttressed legs in Reykjavik, long bamboo canes as big around as your thigh in Shanghai."

"I'll put my back into helping work the rice harvest, and pick tea and mangoes."

"Farmers who tax the trucks and buses by placing sheaves of rice on the tarmac so that the traffic can do the threshing and the winnowing. Broken-down vehicles are surrounded by dotted lines of large rocks. The latent battle between bus drivers and semi drivers for supremacy over a one-way road."

"My mind will be in high places."

"In Beijing, with a red-walled temple or a palace in the background, Chinese people dressed in plain blue put their hatless heads through face-sized cutouts in boards painted with noble characters, knights and princesses, for a souvenir photo."

"I'll see societies that are proud of their harmony."

"In India, I saw the hammer and sickle freshly painted on walls everywhere, whereas in Europe the entire communist world was fiercely erasing them, and in this same setting I saw farmers harvesting rice with their very real sickles and stone breakers preparing the stone for cobbled roads with their very real hammers, each one in his place, not united in the daily struggle of life, contrary to what was being stated by the profusion of those symbols."

"I'll study the lives of women."

"The unskilled female construction workers carry ten bricks on their head: they place the first one on the head, then a second crossed on top of it: they dress their heads by means of a two-armed gesture, as a dancer would make a *couronne*, their hands joining together above their heads, two more bricks, then two more, then two more, then one last one as a capstone . . ."

"But no, as far as I'm concerned, I want to see what is exceptional . . . I want to see the poor dying in the street, I want to see the most beautiful landscapes in the world, I want to be invited into a clean house, and I want to meet the most talented musicians on street corners."

"A turtle in a tub. Two cockroaches in a shower. A thousand ants cleaning up a worm cadaver in two minutes."

"I'll see a lion, a tiger, a jackal. I'll be attacked by a naja cobra, and a gharial. I'll rescue a child from the claws of a condor."

"Get in a fight with a taxi driver over three bucks. Watch naked torsos wash their cloths in gray water. But who will wash the water? Leave your shoes there to go inside Notre-Dame-des-Douleurs, drop them off at the Omeyades coat check. Take off your shirt to go inside the Trichur temple. Put it back on for the sanctuary of Guadaloupe. Will they be reunited with the body? I like churches, especially when they're visited by a solitary infidel."

"I'll cross town on foot. I have the time. I'll walk in the shade. There will be species of birds that have never been seen before. The elephants will mate in front of me."

"A raven lives in Saint-Georges's cupola and flies around the iconostasis, grazing the heads of worshipers. It's hot. It's raining. The earth's crust smokes. Nothing happens, and it's great. We get on the bus on the left side because it drives on the left. The driver boards on the right. Three saintly images side by side in triptych above the dashboard: Kaaba, Vishnu, and Christ."

"I'll see a riot. I'll hear mines go off, far away from the mortars. I'll go to prison. I'll have a fever. I'll risk my life. I'll pierce my tongue with my knife without bleeding."

"I'm a good sleeper."

Odile grabs his hand again.

"I don't want to sleep and let the hours waste away … Is that what you're suggesting we do? At least you aren't sugaring the pill for me … Why would you want me to leave in any case? I would get bored right away."

"You need to leave those you love at least once in your life to see the effect it has."

"Have you left someone before?"

"Someone broke my heart by begging me to leave."

"Who?"

"My girlfriend."

Hans slowly pronounces the word "girlfriend." He doesn't say "m'girlfriend" in one breath. He detaches, just barely, the syllables: "my girl friend."

"How did you treat her?"

"Terribly."

"They'll search your bag at the border."

"My bag . . . Let me touch you, just one gentle touch, I'm begging you! Lean forward and I'll simply brush my fingers along your back."

"No."

"I insist. You'll regret it otherwise."

"No."

"Oh, I won't limit myself to the back. My hand will take the whole tour, gently, without giving you a start. I'll describe each station to you. You know them better than I do . . ."

"That isn't certain."

"So, is that a yes?"

"Your hand is too big. So, no."

Odile is altogether surprised with the excuse that she provides, forcing a smile. She expects Hans Martin to answer that if his hands are bigger, then they're that much better at . . . I don't know what. But the big hand falls back down. He gives up right there, vanquished.

"Well, I guess that's good-bye then."

He gets up, crosses the aisle and sits down ten rows behind her. He closes his eyes, choosing to disappear into an instantaneous sleep.

The bus is in Villefranche. The bus has already been stopped for a few minutes in Villefranche. Odile lets herself go suddenly. She crosses her arms in front of her face. Hans Martin slowly emerges from his universe. He's dragging his feet, his only wish being to go back.

She flips up the armrest so as to have both seats all to herself. She lies down in the fetal position in the square that he's warmed up. She's very fragile, after all. All of the scenery, the entire world, are now imprinted with an absence. The smile cracks. Odile feels herself draining of color. She feels dirty.

She cries, a pussycat whose boots are shined by no one, a traitor who has foregone a taste of love and is now trying to hate herself for it.

Villefranche is the end of the line. My beautiful bus has filled its assigned spot at the bus depot adjacent to the train station. Basile has let go of his steering wheel. He has finally left his seat to stretch his legs, take a piss, wash his hands, and turn in his cash box. I could also get off the bus but I think to myself, "what good would that be?" I haven't given up lying in wait. We have a one-hour break before heading back to the place we left from. Nothing will have changed; it will be the same scenery in the other direction, in the beautiful winter afternoon sunlight. A brief inspection of the bus must be completed, a wipe of a rag on the headlights and the rearview mirrors. Basile checks the blinkers in a ticket office window that reflects an image of the vehicle. He does a little brake check on the way out.

The bus is getting old. Basile makes note of it to himself. It's no longer brand-new: on the undercarriage, rust is discreetly overtaking the joints. The tires are wearing too, but tires can be replaced. When the other drivers see him on the road and say hello with a little honk of the horn, they no longer say to themselves out of the jealousy that they felt at one time: look, there's Basile with his new bus, that lucky devil! That lucky devil has now become part of the crowd.

Basile will soon be done with his routine. What can be done about the idleness and the emptiness? He makes his way back to the passenger cabin, anxious to say something to Odile, or rather to hear a word from Odile . . . to hear what she has to say about what that young man wanted from her, that guy who she sent packing, who left her without further ado, and to find out what his name is.

When Basile sets foot in the passenger cabin once again, his eyes deceive him. He's sure that Hans has left the bus. He doesn't spot Odile, who's lying frozen numb in her little ball. The seats hide her from view. That will have to be fixed. I also take part in hiding her, since what interests me most at this moment in *My Beautiful Bus* is the emptiness that takes hold of Basile, just as it did with Odile, this moment when he feels the onset of all the pain that he has suppressed by delaying his discovery of what was happening in one of the rearview mirrors.

And so here's Basile, a broken-down vehicle of a man who, pshhhh, closes his door to potential intruders and rests his head on the large steering wheel as if he were staring down at the ethereal image of an ideal Odile reflected upward from the bottom of a well. He feels a pit in his stomach formed by the gap between him and Odile, a distance that he believes is growing. She's probably gone. He's sure that she's gone. She's gone. There's no use in knowing for sure. She won't come back. All of his vitality and purpose drain from him.

"But why," thinks Basile, "why aren't I able to be just as

fascinated with the indicator lights on my dashboard as I am with the presence, or the absence, of a woman? Why is it that my ability to experience happiness and suffering, the extremities of feelings, depend on the unknowable? I've never understood her. Why can't I feel the ecstasy of her touch forever, endlessly, a repeating round trip, like a bus line, endlessly, endlessly, endlessly, endlessly, while time stands still, a round trip of the seasons? Odile ... I will always desire you, without ever knowing how to have you. You do what you want. But me, I stir up my unhappiness every time specific words suddenly involve an aversion coefficient: dress, marriage, skirt, perfume, panties, my wife, belly, anti-wrinkle cream, waxing, underarms and bikini, periods, marriage, dress ... all of those words associated with the body that kills you, but that at the same time is the rock of your life, its sunshine and its blank slate. And I know this from a reliable source: I know that I bring Odile nothing but unhappiness."

After a long moment of depression, Basile sits up straight. From what he can tell, Odile still hasn't come back. He decides to head off in search of her anyway, without saying a word to me or the three passengers who have already boarded, having trusted their routine and what's written on the pediment: DIRECTION CHÂTILLON, a return to its initial point of departure. Basile zips off on the wrong road ten minutes after the scheduled departure time, making the gears grind and the engine roar. From what the passengers can remember, this is the first time that this has happened on this bus.

Pshhhh.

He left without closing the bus door. The travelers start to get worried. They grip the handles in front of them or the armrests beside them. They anxiously ask their driver questions, and it's one of the passengers, the one closest to him, who answers in his place, as a mother superior would answer for her priest, who has other souls to whip.

"He has an errand to run, that's for sure . . ."

"But I paid to go the other direction . . ."

"Well, this will be a little detour then!"

"But I don't have time for a detour!"

"If we were on the train, I'd pull the alarm cord."

Disapproval sets in. Someone comes to the front to tap on the driver's shoulder. So, Basile listens and pulls himself together. He pauses. This isn't how he's going to find her again, by setting off blindly. He finally decides to turn around and hastily finds his way back to the bus station in Villefranche. Odile will be there waiting on a bench, busy reading. She will be waiting for Basile to come look for her, turning the pages in a way that reveals a bit of distress. Basile will tactfully say:

"I'm sorry, come here, come back into my kingdom, I'm going to do what I can to distract you. I'm way behind and have far too many slip-ups to earn forgiveness for. Flowers! We'll have to bring flowers! Food and fresh water! We must load up with barrels of flour, herring and all sorts of dried meat, salt, and citrus fruits . . . And road maps, maps that stretch beyond our borders . . . Vacation! Vacation!"

Just as Basile pulls into his stop again, Hans Martin stretches out his gigantic limbs and Odile sits up from behind her hiding place. "What happened?" asks her innocent expression. The three travelers stagger off the bus, as if exiting a roller coaster after an adrenaline rush. They would go to the office to file a complaint if it weren't closed. They come back to the bus to interrogate the driver again. But Basile only has eyes for Odile. Her face doesn't give away her fatigue, she keeps it in the depths of her eyes, those eyes he knows well. Reassured, Basile abruptly makes up his mind.

We're going on vacation. You'll see . . . it'll be a coup d'état, an overthrow of the state's responsibilities. We'll go on vacation, a real vacation. We've never known what that really means. We'll exhaust ourselves. We'll rest.

Hans has a smirk on his face, which Odile can't see but which she can sense behind her back. He has taken out some trail mix from his satchel. He eats.

The sign on the front of the bus has changed, and from now on it indicates SPECIAL LINE. Whoever knows how to read will get off if he fancies or won't get on. Others will decide to stay on the bus out of apathy or sheer curiosity, because they don't have anything better to do.

Basile takes apart ten rows of seats in such a way that a square opens up in the middle of the bus. He puts two pairs of seats back into place as best as he can, but flipped around: with the backs in the same direction the bus moves—a lounge for chatting. It completely changes the ambiance of the place, which at the same time becomes more spacious and more intimate.

Basile has reimbursed those who have asked for a refund out of his own pocket, rounding up. From now on, the trip is free for those who board the bus, as an indifferent nod from the driver testifies. He doesn't care about receipts. But you have to be ready. Ready for what? We're ready, we have the provisions and clothes necessary to face any season. Hans, Odile, Basile, me, surprised, curious, and more attentive than ever to what must be seen, and ready. Four of us comfortably occupy the space of fifty seats.

Soon, from what remains of his clear conscience as a professional, Basile won't miss one stop on a line that he doesn't know on the way toward Clermont. Those who are waiting are dumbfounded:

"But I've never seen you around here before."

"What's special about this line?"

"Are you going to Villers, or Chaumont?"

"To Saint-Martin?"

"La Neuville?

"Viry?"

Every newcomer wonders if the driver has lost his tongue, but doesn't dare to ask about it directly.

"It's free? Well, I'll be darned! That happens less and less often these days!"

"Alright then, I'd better make the most of it."

"Something about this seems suspicious to me."

You either get on or you don't, it doesn't matter to me.

Basile is so excited to be liberating himself from his usual route like this. He can tell that Odile is breathing freely now. She has put her boots back on. She has come closer to him, in the bus, to better appreciate the situation. She stands up, holding on with one hand to the horizontal bar above, and speaks to the driver. She even tenderly caresses his neck, in defiance of the clearly written rules. She advises him about the way when they come across a detour. You can tell that she's making an effort. She's sad.

"You know . . . I feel weary. I think that some gear in my machine is broken. I don't have any willpower. But you're thoughtful with your idea of a trip . . . What good is it to leave now, though? It's too late. I would prefer it if you talked to me a bit about us."

Lie down in the back . . .

"But no!"

I'm taking you on vacation, you'll see, I'm taking you . . . to Paris. You used to love Paris so much and I stopped you from going back there. We'll go see our daughter. We'll take the long way there.

"I'm not sure that I want to . . ."

You'll see.

"What will I see?"

We're going to make up for lost time.

Hours and days go by, days and weeks. For the first time since we embarked, we've started counting the days.

We've started noting down the facts. There are many parallel counts: the one of days gone by, and the one of the days remaining ahead before the likely end of the trip, when my beautiful bus's tank will have run dry. The week-count and the month-count; the day-count was thrown off by an office clock, a clock that I spotted through a window, which had taken its liberties in passing the new year on its own accord: it displayed the date as December 33; the minute-count was thrown off by two electronic clocks in a repair shop sitting side by side, one of them displaying 8:25 PM in red numbers and the other, in white numbers, 8:41 PM. I didn't know what to do with these six minutes emptied of substance or with these two obscure supernumerary days added without explanation to the usual 365. No tour guide had warned me of these time accidents, and the waves of doubt that they've cast on my convictions have yet to be resolved.

We've crossed over plains and villages, towns that go dead at noon, like when night falls over the tropics, we've seen the harvests of wheat and grapes, the newly plowed fields, and more hay bales. People in a garden . . . it's unclear what they're doing, apparently nothing. We don't have the time to dwell on the reason for their lack of activity. Waves of odors drift our way, factory smells, biscuits, chocolate, tobacco, and chemical fertilizer. Right now the bus is following a train through a valley, matching its speed and direction, while in the opposite direction a thousand migratory birds fly overhead. The landscape changes quickly and many times drastically over the course of a day on the road.

I stare at a large plowed field that stretches as far as the eye can see, fresh. A car is stopped on a tractor path with its trunk open, gaping. The car is empty and no one is around, as far as the eye can see.

We drive by.

Prairies followed by prairies. The little white piles in the distance, are they animals or scattered boulders? That cloud looks like a whale. Yes, it's definitely a whale. The forests we go through vegetate. Or a camel now. Young fruit trees wait patiently in a row.

Pretty soon we're going through a village again. It's market day. Odile peers down into a convertible stopped at a red light. A woman sitting in the passenger's seat leans her elbow on the door and has her two knees propped up toward her face, with her thighs showing. Their eyes meet, they size each other up, and they give each other a friendly look. Odile wants to steal her long thighs, and steal the driver's hand that's deep in her lap. What's a woman when a woman looks at her? What's a woman when a man looks at her? I wonder because while I look at the stranger, I also look at her as if I were watching a heroine in a silent film, perceiving only her form, her reputation, not so different from me than any man could be: she's someone else, some other body that's not tied to me by any other circuit than a look. The arm placed on the door with the window rolled down is bare because the three-quarter-length sleeve has been rolled all the way up to the collarbone: a little preoccupation with tanning . . . All of the curves are curves right where they need to be, even though at the local level they are far from fragmentary perfections. They impose that simple perfection of the whole that makes up a complete, moving, abandoned, body—a holder of a nonchalant gaze and of a reverie, a holder of a troubling ability (but I didn't ask anything from her!) to make me think about another woman, who's no stranger to me, and who I miss, and whether she misses me or not I can't say, and whose body is unlike any others, and who I could pick in the thickest darkness from among two-and-a-half billion women.

In Beaumont, we drank wine from Châteauneuf and talked with a motorcyclist, well into his fifties, who was attempting a Tour de France along a predetermined circuit—another organized trip—one that roughly draws the shape of a big heart on a road map.

In Villiers, Basile has to halt: something worries him, something having to do with the motor. False alarm, all it needs is lubrication, a need that forces us to take a two-hour break, letting our eyes wander around an indolent garage.

Basile takes roads that become narrower and narrower. Driving past an oncoming vehicle becomes impossible. Basile drives slowly, being careful to spare the hedgehogs, butterflies, and little insects.

And Basile, Basile! What good is this detour to an abandoned train station with shattered windows? Grass sprouts between the rails and grows high over onto the road. An old train wagon is inhabited. It's a wasteland. A guy approaches the bus, begs, and laughs, showing the few teeth he has left: "It's to get something to eat, not to drink."

Basile hands him some change.

And why, Basile, why do you stop a little further along if not to make a stranger happy: a sick sheep not looking quite up to par is brought on board, off to the veterinarian. Odile strokes her hand through the greasy wool in an attempt to soothe the sick animal.

Odile isn't really happy. Basile has nevertheless done the necessary to distract her. They have seen the ocean, taken the waters, and eaten delicacies. They have twisted and turned around the entire country, have met travelers on foot from another century, surprised by this godsend: a driver who'll take them where they want to go, all the way to their doorstep.

Basile drives much faster than he ever has before. He drives at top speed sometimes, as if he wanted to spare his loved one from landscapes that don't seem worthy of her, and lingers on other choice moments where the gaze extends into the distance.

Basile has carried us across borders, has led us through the heat and the cold, through deserts, over mountains, through the middle of terrible droughts and under torrential rains. Through my window, I can make out immense cities where populations cram in to better deal with the misery amid the excess of noise, filth, and poverty. I see modest villages made of earth, it would almost be dishonest to deem them weatherproof, and on the other hand there are tall and quarrelsome cities where the night is conquered by manmade light. I make out people of all colors, satiated people and starving people of all colors, people affected by every kind of pain, morsels of beauty, and shards of ugliness.

The bus is put on the deck of a boat: I sail the warm seas sprinkled with immobile islands, cold seas with mountains of icebergs that drift slowly. Never do I want to get off my beautiful bus, where I experience a timeless torpor during the vast majority of the trip; never do I want to get off, so long as the destinies of my two *-iles*, Odile and Basile, have not been fulfilled.

Hans slept, read, and watched. Sometimes he wrote in a little white hardcover notebook with his mouth half open. His lips moved. He would look as if he were suffering. And then once again he would be carefree. He slept easily no matter what the weather was like outside, no matter what the time of day, or the position he was in.

We watched as the light dimmed in the cabin. Basile installed a makeshift screen and asked us to pull our window curtains closed. Without my beautiful bus altering its course or delaying its progress along its fastidious route, we watched, more than once, a film that played without the sound, since we didn't have headphones to plug into the armrests of our seats.

The camera (just like the projector) is set in the bus, and rolls down the road through the opening credits. But soon it decides to liberate itself from the rectilinear road, from the smooth surface packed down by steamrollers, cambered by engineers, and repaved by public road-maintenance crews. My beautiful bus, light as can be, drifts off the pavement. Using my jacket as a makeshift drop-cloth, I block the light, which might overexpose the film, from coming in through the window. I pause to watch the paved ground drift away through the window. We have taken a dirt trail, a shortcut, which will itself need to be abandoned, in turn, for a path. The bus no longer has windowpanes. The wind whips one side of your face through the openings. We move forward over a cushion of grass. The movie is in color. I see nothing but green while we're in the temperate climates. Soon I see yellow. If I were a painter, I would pour out a lot of yellow on this twisting and turning course. The wilderness is empty, uninhabited. My beautiful bus has slowed down. It glides silently along in the unmoving forest. Not a soul stirs; no forest ranger's cabin is in sight, and not a single farm.

Without my noticing, a man has boarded the moving bus, he's a guide with big confident eyes who tells me everything I should see, promises me flora in all the colors of the rainbow: irises, blueberries, soft ferns, buttercups and marigolds, bougainvillaea; promises me fauna in a full range of sizes: ants and anthills, field mice, rats and badgers, foxes and feral dogs, eagles, all the birds in the sky, little buffalos, a bear ... But there's no trace of insects and the grass is yellow and sparse. I smile condescendingly, unwilling to believe these promises for one second unless the guide can tell me who these wild animals listed in the credits belong to: a hyena was seen near the large banyan tree on the twelfth of September, 1990! An anteater on the thirteenth, and a puma on the sixteenth. The bus has stopped on the edge of the forest with the savanna in sight, shimmering in the heat. Not one animal sound can be heard coming from the forest, no trumpeting from the elephants we were promised; not a lark chirping as I observe the rapidly darkening sky. I sit behind clods of dirt, my hideout ... Nothing at the foot of the banyan tree that itself is sitting upright, nothing in the high grass pops its head up. Nothing in the pine trees. Nothing in the stubble fields. The guide's smile says, "It's always like this on the first day." His movements are too calm to roll a cigarette, light it, and smoke it.

The next day, I saw the animals from the second day, those

that definitely had been there yesterday but that I had frightened away—or maybe it's that I didn't know how to see them because I hadn't slowed down yet. They weren't exceptional sightings as far as the whole animal kingdom is concerned, but my astonishment matched my disappointment from the evening before when I'd fallen asleep empty-handed. I managed to get my fill by playing hide-and-seek with two black woodpeckers with red skullcaps while they prospected in the trunk of a eucalyptus tree. They passed along a melodious message laden with a bad sense of irony, tapping it with their beaks on a hollow branch, the same tune heard by a marquis's brother as the carillon played in the distance, when he was a prisoner of Vincennes. Yes, Sade's brother:

I pity you, I pity you
Only your end awaits you
It's only dust, only dust.

I awoke very early in the morning on the third day, convinced that the morning hours were the most favorable for serious encounters. I wanted to get off my beautiful bus and pluck up the courage to get a closer look at the buffalos that were wading through a marshland. The guide advised me not to, but I didn't heed him. I put on some waders and swung a small sack over my shoulder. I brought a bottle full of water that had been boiled. I had a sweatshirt for when night fell, and some binoculars. I pretended to be Goofy, the Disney character, whose adventures I had recently clipped out of an issue of *Mickey Parade*: a two-lane road split by a solid white line is surrounded by a mountainous backdrop. There's a road sign on the right side of the road:

DEER

CROSSING

And so Goofy sets off across the road, placing his two thumbs on his temples and extending his disproportionately large fingers outward, imitating a set of antlers and points.

Having reassured myself with this makeshift camouflage, I followed my instincts. I knew that there had to be an animal out there for me, one that was just as unique as I expected, one that I would have to track down until nightfall. A dreadful feeling stayed with me, a grain of salt lingered in my excitement, a feeling caused by leaving my beautiful bus behind, in the distance, similar perhaps to what you feel when you leave the home you grew up in for the first time. Walking cautiously, my gaze was no longer caught by the peacocks, mountainous anthills, and herons, which had already satisfied my eyes. The buffalos had become average everyday cows. When I heard the sound of breaking branches in the forest, I knew that it was a troupe of elephants doing exactly what was expected of them without complaining.

I spoke to myself aloud: head into the forest, leave its all too well-known borders. Go where no one ever goes, because deprived of water; easy prey like impalas, antelopes, and agoutis penetrate the depths of the forest only once they're already withered. Once inside, the forest opened to a clear sky above, although the grass was high. As I walked, I tried to flatten down the least possible amount of grass, to avoid making my passage through the blades noticeable. And at the same time, I was conscious of how futile my precautions were, for I could do nothing about my scent, not knowing how to smell it, nor how to make it unnoticeable.

Having arrived at a location that I thought to be sufficiently central in this forbidden territory (I thought that if I went further, I would only end up getting closer to the borders of the forest, further decreasing my chances of finally seeing a wildcat, for it was a wildcat that I was looking for as tourist booty, something to brag about), I sat down. The grass immediately seemed higher and I waited for hours. Such a silence—I'd never known silence before. It was as if I were out fishing on a big peaceful lake, waiting for a fish to break the surface, darting up from the bottom to satiate itself with a star.

Without making a sound, I rose to my feet and moved forward into the suffocating humidity. The ground gave way under my step and once again I found myself in muddy water, but this time I was covered in leeches and got water up my nose. I wanted to fight through, but was unable to make my way out of this warm basin alone and the pernicious urge to give in to drowning became harder and harder to resist.

I muse on a version of the fable in which this episode has a happy ending: the dialogue between the naked young miller's son and his sly partner as he concludes his decisive bathing ritual: the young man is dressed anew in expensive garments. Finally, the king's manservant brings him the missing piece of the attire suitable for a marquis who's out on a stroll: a pair of boots that will once and for all transform him into Carabas. But boots, he has never worn boots before. His feet aren't made for these garments that seem like a prison to him.

"May I at least be allowed to slip in a hay lining . . ."

"Why master, you mustn't even think of such a thing! If you do that you would give away your bumpkin nature, your virgin nature! Put them on, come on now! It isn't all that bad! Believe me, I'm used to them. Surely you notice that the princess is blind and harmless, that her father, the king, is a drunken imbecile and that his court is full of cowardly worms. Bare feet are reserved for begging monks and all sinless creatures, straw is for country bumpkins, and hay is for petty bourgeois. Walk, walk! Don't give in to worrying about your health because of your blistered feet. You have nothing to fear. It's high time you ruled the world beneath your feet. Just one last little effort, go on, and soon you will owe me everything. All I ask for in return is the totality of your love."

I was rescued from the water during the night. I had already given up all hope, all of my senses had dulled, my skin had become waterlogged, and my blood had been sucked. My savior was amphibian. She was a white tiger, a small one, a miniature version the size of a child. Her hind legs were strong and worn, and the glistening white stripes on her body freed themselves from her matte coat, also short and white, following the caprices of the lunar gleam: a queen of the night. I didn't know whether to fear her or lie underneath her, a Milady de Merteuil (a chimera made of two pseudo-sister chimeras that somberly illuminate *Dangerous Liaisons* and *The Three Musketeers*), whose cuddliness, whose ability to grant me an immense pleasure, I simply wanted to believe, while at the same time I was clearly aware of her intrinsic ferociousness, cleverness, and capacity for remorseless revenge.

At this point in the film, the picture faded to white and I sadly came back to the vehicle. My cloths, stiff with mud, had dried out while I walked, and their rubbing and scraping inflamed my skin. At this point in the film, Basile always slows my beautiful bus down, it's beyond him not to. He grimaces and grits his teeth. He wishes that he could simply will the film to rewind back to the precise instant of the apparition. Basile brakes to avoid running into a chimera.

Outside, the fog is thick and at times it's as if we were drifting along above a flock of white sheep, a sea of clouds, or a sea of waves. A young woman passes through the aisle to kindly offer us biscuits and tea from her thermos.

When the fog lifts, I recognize a familiar landscape: delicate undulating hills segmented by wide, deep grooves.

How much time has gone by since my beautiful bus radically deviated from its designated course? The duration of a long journey, perhaps of an around-the-world-trip along a random route. Basile has thrown other seats overboard; those that remain can be counted on a single hand. Little by little, we've made ourselves comfortable. My beautiful bus is a caravan. Hans Martin has taken root. He and Odile have talked and talked and talked. I witnessed a furtive kiss. Basile has become a bulimic kilometer eater, pulling out all the stops to show Odile the most prestigious sites when they present themselves: Tassili n'Ajjer, Borobudur and the Ming Dynasty tombs, the Ise mountain range, Easter Island, Mita, Monument Valley, Ultima Thule, the Faroe Islands, the Giant's Causeway, Mont Saint-Michel . . . The famous sites are always the most disappointing and I don't know why. I wonder why.

"I can tell you why," says Hans Martin, waking and stretching. "I've known why since the day I decided to return to the place where I was disappointed. You have to go to the famous site twice. The second time is less disappointing. It's better to visit each site twice and therefore half as many sites in all. Morning and evening. Once one day, and then once the following day. You have to sleep there, so that falling asleep, dreaming, and waking up all happen in the same place. You have to eat there, so that digestion occurs on site. You have to see more than one sun there."

I look at Hans, who's finally talking to me, and smile at him, to communicate my agreement. Hans has slept well. He's very relaxed. He scratches his chin where a blond beard has discreetly grown in. Basile has spotted him. Basile is sulking.

"What I see in a trip," continues Hans, "isn't the satisfying of expectations. That would lead to outright disappointment. 'To see Naples and die' means to die from having so badly wanted to see an idea of Naples and to die of disappointment. I want the Naples that I see to be a departure point for considering what Naples might be, each and every Napolitano and each crack in every façade, every *fumarole* off in the distance and every . . . A trip is a launching pad."

Are you writing a treatise on trips? You seem like you know how to travel . . . that you know how to travel better than others. It's irritating. You're pontificating, my friend.

"Every stop on a trip is the beginning of a line, not an endpoint. A trip is endless. I'll only take a few of the potential lines. I'm happy to discover one that's fertile. And you know something . . . the one that yields isn't always the one that you anticipated."

Hans is talking out loud. He's saying this to me, but he wants Odile to hear too.

"One day, I went to Craonne, in the Champagne region, with my father, who lived out his later years immersed in generals' wartime memoirs. There were crosses everywhere, planted in even rows. The cannon thundered rhythmically, boom, boom, boom, ominous explosions interrupted by moments of silence that allowed the threat sufficient time to reverberate. There was a lot of smoke. But not enough to block the trenches from view, the earth cut open by trenches and shell craters. The earthworms and moles had given up, as had the plows. Boom, screams, boom, screams, and so on. The smoke had thickened when a favorable gust cleared the air just enough for me to make out a gigantic Prussian, dressed like an Empire general or a coalition leader, soberly leaning over a rotting cat carcass nailed to a wooden cross by its four limbs. He puts his gold-hilted sword back in its sheath. A beautiful and rare sight of a general who wonders to himself, "Does a people have the right to change the intimate and rational manner by which another people wants to rule its material and moral existence?" He has nevertheless emerged victorious from a raging battle, and on the way back home, as I followed him like a page boy, sitting in his sedan, he opens his favorite book from his countryside library, the book that he hasn't finished figuring out even after a hundred readings."

Which book?

"A fable. You know . . . my own story, it starts with my backpack, just a small thing . . . and then another bag inside my backpack. But remember when Odile asked me a question about my bag, she wanted to ask something banal, a trivial question, an especially non-engaging one, and now she might drop everything to help me carry my package to the ends of the earth!"

But why do you stay aboard my beautiful bus? Does Odile really interest you?

"Maybe."

Who is she?

"I don't know what she is. I wonder what she's capable of being. But what about you, what are you doing aboard? Why did you get on in the first place?"

Oh me, when I take a seat on a bus, provided that it rolls along, I'm happy. I have a smile on my face. That's the extent of it. And I watch. I'm watching Basile who's watching Hans with an evil eye. Odile sees this look. I haven't taken one photograph through my window; I don't keep any portraits of Odile in my black box.

Odile doesn't express one bit of gratitude to Basile throughout the unfathomable duration of the trip. She's simply proud that Hans Martin is still there at her side. As for Basile, he's bitter. He has aged. He has shrunken into his seat a little. The sides of my beautiful bus are completely covered in dried mud, but Basile doesn't care. She's the only thing he worries about anymore.

It's clear to me that Odile and Basile will never go back to their house, that they will never return to the past.

Odile decides to stretch out on the four seats remaining in the very back of the bus above the motor, near Hans, who has settled in on the floor. She has sadly removed her ankle boots. She stares at Hans. He waits. Seeing this, Basile's chin begins to tremble. He accelerates the approach toward a larger city. An arrow indicates, "Clermont 26 km." His head swells, he has trouble breathing. Poor Basile. We have to get there as soon as possible, drive through the suburbs, and make it to the center. He doesn't know why. Perhaps to take the road to Paris again— ALL DESTINATIONS—if it isn't too late . . . Basile is such an enigma to Odile. She searches. She remembers their first trip, runs through the sequence of events of his wait by the fountain in Paris: the cold weather, the little clouds of fog, like the mute smudges that mark the mirror held in front of you, for a brief moment providing evidence that you're alive.

Odile doesn't understand how she has lived so many years without understanding this moment.

Odile looks down at the floor. It looks to me as if she's watching a little mouse. She's waiting for me to give her a convincing explanation, the one I've been looking for since the very first moments I spent on my beautiful bus and which I haven't found, lazy as I am, and bewitched as I am by Odile and her fleeting charm. Since the puss without boots is bootless, she can ask for my advice. She looks at my shod feet. She drinks up my consoling words without believing them, those words that I would like from the bottom of my heart to speak to her, a speech that I steal from her own abilities and that I address primarily, I'm aware, to myself. No, Basile hadn't been looking for another woman. Or if indeed he had been looking for another woman, it wasn't to replace Odile, who occupied his mind entirely, and so much so that Odile found herself without any room to breathe. There must have been another, more obscure reason, one that words can't express, which Basile might just take with him to his grave.

For twenty-five years, Odile endured the choice of civil peace on the common ground shared with her partner. She was helped along by the presence of a desired child, a cumbersome marvel, from whom she was unable to hide any of her mortification and who consequently ended up holding it against her mother for accepting the straitjacket.

Odile decides right here and now, sitting right next to us, to write to her daughter. My darling, I want to ask something from you, something important, sweetie. I would like to ask you not to come back so soon to see us. You have to work hard so that you can surround yourself with people who will be successful. With us, I can tell, you're afraid of wasting your time. That's okay. I really do understand. Don't feel ashamed about not coming back. The time will come when you will feel like taking a break by coming home to us, you'll feel like taking your mind off of things, rediscovering a few of those things that bore you right now. You need to work a lot, you know. Your father feels the same way I do. Don't come back unless you hear otherwise. Isn't that right, Basile, don't you feel the same? Of course, I'm in the middle of writing to our little girl, I want to tell her that you feel the same way I do. I'm telling her how much we miss her and I'm asking her to come see us as soon as she can. I'm asking her to make an effort, for you. I'm telling her that she needs to come home and take a break, that she will only work better afterwards. Isn't that right, sweetie, aren't you going to come see us, hello, I'm having trouble hearing you, yes, your dad is here, right next to me, and he agrees. I'll call you back. You wouldn't have a two-and-a-half-franc stamp, would you, Basile? Yes, I'll give him a hug for you, and I'm sending you one from him. You've got such firm hugs! And what about me, now, do you have a kiss left for me?

My beautiful bus put the letter in the mail. At the same stop, it bought the paper. It got back on the road in the late autumn scene, slowed by wide loads, wagons full of beets, and the fog. Slowed by the succession of war memorials that symbolically bar the road as a physical reminder of trenches, interventions and counter-attacks, assassination attempts, sabotages, settlings of scores, gassings, the wounded, the avenged, the sold, the captives . . .

The wide plains are full of dull colors. To smile a bit, why not look forward to the future rapeseed fields, those beautiful diamonds of bright yellow, the soft budding wheat, and the poppies?

Basile doesn't reach out his hand, doesn't stretch out his finger as he usually would. He doesn't point out a sparrow hawk listening on a telephone wire or the flight of a buzzard, which describes a threatening circle.

Basile slows down, taking into account the heavy rain, which turns the road slick. On the left, I see a sort of artificial plateau. It's a public garbage dump. Scattered all around, shreds of bags and newspaper pages cling to the sides of the heap. They're all objects with memories that are weightless and without legend, clinging to the bulging clumps and brambles.

The road is permanent. The road never stops. The view out the window is dark and banal: a wide desolate plain, trees without leaves, a few dead elms.

Suddenly, situated twenty meters off to the right from an intersection with a stone cross, an outline of an artificial hill takes shape. It's a silo full of silage, a bunker silo, covered with a plastic tarp that is itself covered with old black tires. Underneath, a subtle mixture is fermenting that will be used as livestock feed. Basile puts his brakes on and pulls onto the shoulder.

Pshhhh . . .

Basile:

I'll keep going if he gets off.

Odile:

"He's not getting off. Unless I go with him."

Odile loses it. She jumps up out of her seat. She steps forward.

I want Odile to remain standing next to the driver, trembling all over, I want her to talk to him, to smoke, and spit, to be alive, to claw him on the neck and make him get back on the road.

Pshhhh ...

Basile has adjusted his rearview mirror toward the roof. He has folded his left side-view mirror inward. He doesn't look behind him anymore, and he hardly looks much more in front of him, at the road. He drives while staring at Odile for long moments. He tears along the deserted road.

Odile's waiting for something, a last chance, a lifeline that will float by within her reach, something that she can grab onto. She waits for a word, for him to talk to her, for him to tell her ... Instead, he continues onward, driving at top speed, only making the movements necessary to drive.

"Will you tell me ..."

What?

"Before I say good-bye to you ..."

Good-bye?

"Farewell, if you prefer ... before I say farewell to you. You see, I'm done with us. I feel as if I'm going to swell up and burst. I must be all puffy."

Odile's face is completely pink. She's far away.

"Will you tell me about ..."

Yes.

And he remains silent.

"Now."

What?

"What you've done to me?"

Huh? What do you mean?

"What did you want from me?"

What do you mean . . . nothing.

"Come on, what did you want from me?"

That you be . . .

"That I be what?"

That you be . . . forever.

"What does that mean?"

Nothing more than that . . . that you be forever.

"Explain. Go on, tell me the rest of it!"

I wanted to remove you from time.

"What happened in Paris?"

What?

"Who did you call, on that Easter eve . . ."

No one . . .

"Basile!"

Yes, to the speaking clock.

"I know, but why?"

For no reason.

"Are you kidding me . . ."

I found out what strike of midnight rings at midnight. The third beep of the speaking clock squeezed in between the sixth and the seventh strikes of the bell.

"But why did you want to know that? Why? Did you have a meeting with someone?"

Yes.

"You need to tell me everything. Who did you see at midnight, near the fountain? Tell me now!"

Basile slows down. His hands clench his steering wheel. He grits his teeth. He trembles.

"Who?"

A toad.

"Basile!"

A city toad . . .

Odile is furious.

". . . that you kissed on the mouth . . ."

. . . a city toad that smelled like sewage and medicine. Yes, I kissed it on the mouth.

". . . and it transformed into a beautiful young woman, of course."

No, an ugly old woman.

"Into a witch."

For example.

"Carabosse?"

Hah!

"With a pimple on her nose."

How did you know?

"So then what happened?"

She told me that she would grant me a wish and that in exchange I would have to stay silent. She laughed when she said it. Her mouth was moist and dripping. Her skin was moist. She was sweating. She stank. Her laugh was hollow. I should have been more wary of her laugh. I was too busy thinking about what you had said to me one day, jokingly, that I was going to make you . . . You had said: "Please, be quiet, so that I can stay the way I am . . ." or something like that.

"You're crazy."

I wanted to lift you up off the ground. Hate me, since I've failed.

"I hate you because you've succeeded. It's awful. And so, I've given you everything. Nothing's left for me. You couldn't have found a better way to thank me!"

Odile . . .

Odile starts yelling. She's red and feverish. She isn't angry. She laughs. She's elated. Hans Martin is reading the newspaper with a serious and absent look.

Odile:

"I never asked you for anything. In whose name did you want to reduce me, and with what right? Who gave you permission to . . . ? Who gave you permission to touch me? In the name of love, that's too simple, you kept all of the extremes hidden from me. One person's love is merely the other's unhappiness. One person doesn't understand anything about the other's joy, nothing about the other's sex."

Odile says the word "sex" as if it were the first time that it passed through her lips. She says the word "love," however, as if it were going to be useful again for another affair, for a successful one.

But . . . I know everything about you, Odile, as if I made you. You're everything to me. You're beautiful, solid, and responsible. You are my rock. You are the reason I live. I've become you.

"No way. I can't stand up straight. I'm frivolous. I teeter dangerously. I get swept up by the wind. I'm unrestrained. There's still time left for me to be frivolous. No one is the end of anyone."

You are my end.

"Well, then you're done for, because I've already gotten off."

Is Basile done for? Basile ponders this and no longer wants to insinuate anything. Basile has ceased making an effort to be present, to hold this incomplete position in the dialogue. He won't say anything more about it, even if Odile were to shake him down for reasons and motives, or even wale on him with her fists and tear his overalls to shreds.

It's at this moment that I choose to approach him, to touch his shoulder and take possession of him, so as to be able to say whatever comes to my mind, to sedate Basile a little before his end, to whisper Odile's excuses in his ear (what am I getting myself into?), the sorry story of some childish despair, of a wound . . . Basile, listen to me . . . I grope clumsily for words . . . that long and tall woman with drab hair and boots on . . . Come on, little Basile, no more crying . . . the little cat died while crossing the street without looking. You're going to write to the Department of Transportation and tell them that the road regulations handbook needs to include a sign that says "Caution, crossing of felines very dear to the hearts of little children, slow down."

Slow down . . . Pshhhh . . .

"And don't you follow me . . . you hear! I'd rather not be . . . accompanied. Sorry, Basile, but I'm going to say it again . . . I don't love you. I've moved on."

Hans has hopped off onto the road and has opened the luggage compartment. He already has the giant bag on his back. He waits with his hand out for Odile to come and put her hand in his. She comes over to him. He's already sticking his thumb out. They argue. She wants him to leave the bag there in the ditch, covering it with foliage. He shakes his head no, while smiling. She insists, displaying her lack of discipline. No. She argues.

"You piss me off with your sins of the world!"

He points his finger at the bag while hammering away with replies of no, no. She fights tooth and nail. I don't know how the negotiation will turn out.

My beautiful bus has set off like a bat out of hell. It joins a section of the toll road—that it will soon choose to exit in order to flee a traffic jam. The skies are immense. Who says you don't see any scenery on the toll road? You see skies that are even vaster because they've been underlined by the road.

When at last my beautiful bus gets back on the highway, night is ready to fall. Cities take shape on the outskirts, outposts of the big city loom with lights in the crenels. It's that time of day when everyone leaves the office, the construction site, and the factory. Everyone is out at the same time. Trains pass each other above roads and packed buses. You can count on a red light every few blocks. All along the freeway, huge storefronts line the road, almost like warehouses for Herculean purchases: furniture and tires, garages, gas stations, car dealerships, and lumberyards . . . and a bunch of those abandoned residences that were at one time owned by bourgeois who lived beside a two-lane road that never stopped widening over the course of the century of the automobile.

Basile drives slowly. He's tired. He takes a side road and then stops to let the six o'clock rush go by. He goes into a bistro with his thermos in hand to order a tea, and comes back to the cockpit to offer some to Odile, who isn't there.

Two soaked hitchhikers sagging under the weight of a backpack which is sagging just as much as they are come over to ask him if he happens to be going toward Paris. He's headed there, but in a little bit. With a polite wave, he motions for them to come aboard. Basile would light a wood fire to dry them off and warm them up. He makes do with starting his engine up again and turning the heat on full blast. Basile looks at me as if he were waiting for me to thank him for the distraction that he has provided me with. But I go back inside my shell. I don't want

113

the newcomers to spot me. And so they carry on as if they don't see me, they hide their bag as if they were somewhat ashamed, dirty, damp, rank, and drunk . . . they stay up front with their wet-dog smell, with their backs leaning against the inside walls of the bus. One of them speaks loudly and the other responds quietly. One is leaving; the other is on his way home. One tells about what he's anticipating and the other about what he's bringing back.

It's dark out, the time of day when things quiet down. Everyone has fallen asleep: the two travelers and Basile; but me, I'm only pretending to sleep so that I don't miss anything, sure that this reprieve won't last. The faint glow of Paris completely dominates the heavenly sky.

Basile's going to get back on the road even though there's no hurry. The engine warms up and Basile gives the two side-view mirrors a wipe with a rag. It hasn't stopped raining. The road will continue to be slick, and the visibility will be poor.

It's nighttime, the kind of night that makes for a light sleep, an endless night.

Basile has trouble finding his way back on the highway in the labyrinth of one-way streets. His nervousness takes hold of him again. My, how he has changed! His driving has become so jerky! Will he become an animal among the pack of road-raging maniacs? The windshield wipers sweep furiously. The gears grind. The tires squeak. The brakes are applied harshly. We're only twenty kilometers away from Paris, all of us, Basile, my beautiful bus, the two tourists who haven't completely dried off, and a driver who ran out of gas who knows where to find a gas pump open all night long in Orly. Basile stopped to pick him up. He was waiting hopelessly, on the side of the road in front of a construction site and behind a large apartment building under demolition.

Pshhhh.

"Do I owe you anything?"

Nothing, not even five shillings.

"You're really kind."

There are still two more stoplights. Stop. Basile is in the right lane. A semi has just pulled up next to him on the left. Basile stares the driver down disagreeably. Why is he seated higher up than him? He doesn't like his large size. He doesn't like his flaky, balding head. However, the other driver waves to him like a colleague. Basile gets ready for a breakaway, putting the engine in gear. He wants to leave him in the dust when the light turns green. My beautiful bus slices through the air, its body vibrating with impatience, it flies as it lunges forward. It almost works. The semi wrinkles its nose a few meters behind. But right away there's a two-kilometer-long slope that has to be climbed. The mastodons have proudly committed to climbing the slope, and are soon forced to downshift. The semi gains on us and starts to pass. I see its name appear in huge letters on the tarp covering the metal cargo frame: . . . ORTATION, . . . ANSPORTATION, . . . REL TRANSPORTATION, . . . CANTEREL TRANSPORTATION . . . He catches up to us, and now we are neck and neck in front of a funny looking building on the right with a notched and semispherical tower, it's an observatory. The entry gate is solemn and crested with an inscription depicting a star and the words engraved above it:

AD VERITATEM PER SCIENTIAM

"Toward truth through science," and while the race between the two vehicles becomes increasingly violent as the slope flattens out, a revelation transpires that would be unprecedented, if I hadn't read Raymond Roussel beforehand, if I were unfamiliar with this particular ascent and the reason Basile, after his catastrophe, still had a clear destination, or even better if, being omnipotent, I hadn't premeditated this return and made my beautiful bus take this road instead of another, this particular road that I took on my bicycle for several years to go to and from school, the one that could have accommodated a Versailles, as Louis XIV and André Le Nôtre had once envisioned it, or at least a "royal house," a vague project of Charles Perrault's, this time as the first delegate of the Superintendency of the King's Buildings, who writes that on this hillside "there is an infinite landscape of resources,"[9] this road that adjoins the Viry hamlet, where I was born, where I loved and worked, and where Paquette Le Clerc, Pierre Perrault's wife, Master Charles's mom and Mother Goose, lived and bore her children, who themselves inherited the residence, where Christiaan Huygens, inventor of such things as the pendulum clock, was guest of honor and where he calculated on October 8, 1669, in competition with Claude Perrault, the speed of sound, "180 Parisian lengths per second," where Calvaliere Bernini was invited in May, 1665, by Paul Fréart de Chantelou, on behalf of the king, who in the end wouldn't carry through with his project to extend the Louvre à la I. M. Pei, as if the legendary Raymond Roussel hadn't convinced me right from the origin, and through osmosis within this selfsame place, of the irrepressible logic that

---

[9] Charles Perrault, *Mémoires de ma vie*, première edition intégrale, Paris, 1909.

every work of imagination obeys (as well as life, in short, short as it is), in which all of its elements, which are apparently contiguous, maintain internal continuity, through patterns of rhyme and echo, unconscious patterns, but patterns that are not ends, which are on the contrary opportunities for a literary individual, whose powers of fiction are productive and generative, just as Basile fights with this semi, wheel against wheel, tooth and nail, with the pedal to the metal, double-clutching the accelerations, and I see the wheel right in front of my face, through the window, and I start to wonder what kind of cycloid movement the hubcap bolt I'm focused on is following, and how it would be possible to calculate its movement, and trace its curve on a piece of paper, before I remember in a flash what I already knew and had forgotten, that our Pascal, our Blaise, who wanted to overcome a toothache, strived to resolve a mathematical problem called "la roulette," "the wheel" (which might have had a part in convincing some that he had invented, not the dentist's drill, also known as a "roulette" by some, but the wheelbarrow, at that time also designated by the word "roulette," despite the fact that it had existed well before him!), and it's on this same hillside in Juvisy—perhaps at the precise spot where, 270 years later, Roussel will visit Camille Flammarion who he admired, as Michel Leiris says, "to the point that he contrived a special star-shaped transparent box which he used to conserve a little cake in the same shape which he brought back from a lunch with the renowned astronomer on July 29, 1923 at the Observatory of Juvisy"—two hundred meters away from a tombstone beneath which lie the bodies of four Queneaus, one of them the king of programmed coincidence in the small space of the novel—to such a degree that the characters of *La Dragonne* by Alfred Jarry, after Juvisy, Paris behind them, leave "M. Legay on the right, who practices the profession that is just, subtle, and the sister of death: that of the sandman" (this must be a misprint by Mr. Longuet!)—on this hillside in Juvisy, therefore, where Pascal got the idea[10] to hunch over a question that his predecessors in mathematics, Galileo, Mersenne, had already pondered . . . but which they had left unfinished, to launch an international contest that would give him plenty of trouble.

So Pascal started off with a nail driven into the perimeter of a wheel that he speculated was perfectly circular. No other reason than this motivates me to motivate Basile to drive his bus back to Paris, just when all order in his world is teetering. He desperately wants to close the circle of his love as if the wheel weren't touching the ground, just as every naïve response to the cycloid problem is formulated using this false information about the circle or the right wheel: of course, the movement of the nail in the wooden rim would make a perfect circle if the wheel weren't touching National Route 7, if it weren't engaged in time and space and space-time. But in reality the nail doesn't touch the same spot twice. It advances along the curve drawn by Pascal:

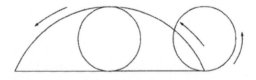

---

[10] At least that's what Jean Anglade claims in his *Pascal l'insoumis* [Pascal the Disobedient], Librairie académique Perrin, Paris, 1988, page 343. I have no idea where he found a quote about this detail. He himself has no clue.

which should be read from right to left.

When talking about the future, you can't think of everything, it's impossible to change everything that must be changed when predicting that something is in a state of change. The wheel isn't set firmly enough on the spatial rug.

What kind of curve have we drawn while floating above the road in my beautiful bus? We're immobile and yet we're moving. The bus transports us.

Basile accelerates. He's on the brink of being passed on his left. He honks furiously and rams his vehicle against the CANTEREL semi. For me, my face glued to the window that is now touching the tarp of the other vehicle, things are becoming worrisome. The two tyrannosauruses brush against one another, spraying an enormous shower of sparks. Some rubber burns during the collision. The brakes smoke. Basile's competitor has had to slow his pace, but he's quickly picking it back up again, and will continue to, since an underpass has just appeared in his lane that's designed to avoid a congested intersection up ahead. He dives under the road with the roof just barely clearing the tunnel ceiling. Basile, however, is forced to remain at ground level. The light is yellow. Oh well, he runs it, which up until yesterday would have been unthinkable, and a hundred meters further he meets back up with his enemy, whose rage has only escalated. Basile resorts to extreme measures: he cuts him off on the left. His opponent has no choice but to slam on the brakes and even change lanes. He veers into the two lanes of oncoming traffic and looses control of his trailer, sending him spinning like a top whose cord has been pulled. What can the car in front of him do to avoid this slap of metal, this backhand blow of a racket that will send it flying in a ball of flames into the front of a store for bathroom fixtures?

So much for our respectful, responsible, and dutiful driver, Basile. In his ferocious race, Basile didn't stop for the cheering, the ovations, the laughs, the jeers, the curses, nor even to help the people in danger. The wounded won't receive any emergency assistance. Basile dives under Orly's runways.

Pshhhh.

He lets out the driver of the gasless car, who is white with fear and no longer knows if he should say thank you, remain silent, or yell at him. Basile speeds off toward Paris, imagining himself at the wheel of an army tank. Time is running out.

He doesn't slow down until he reaches the Porte d'Orléans. Night is already well under way. Paris sleeps, except for a few taxis, an ambulance, and the partygoers who drive fast. And the cops.

Basile makes his way through Paris. The two backpackers are asleep. Basile goes straight. He thinks to himself that he'll soon intersect the Seine and might drive past his daughter's windows above. She's asleep. A young man is in her bed. Basile drives by. He follows a sign: *Hôtel de Ville*. After a few turns in the road, he arrives at Eglise Saint Paul. The little fountain has disappeared. It looks as if there's never been one. The clock on the bell tower has stopped. It says that it's nine thirty, when it's maybe five at the latest. Basile doesn't say anything, but he's doubtful. His eyes take note of the obvious. He doesn't want to recognize anything in Paris.

Pshhhh.

Basile wakes up his passengers. He gets off before them. With a wave of his hand, he says: Paris, the Seine, Notre-Dame . . . He goes to take a peek through the back window to see if

Odile is sleeping. Odile is not there.

Pshhhh.

The night carries on. Lights are scarce through the windows. The pavement glistens, and the sky is dark. A wind is going to start howling, a violent wind which will carry the clouds off to the east in masses. I spot a green municipal sprinkler, which turns itself on and starts drumming away.

Basile crosses the northern boundary of Paris. He dead reckons along a canal. He looks like he knows this area like the back of his hand, even though he's driving aimlessly. He scans the dark sky in an attempt to spot evidence of the rising sun and to enjoy this time of day. He progresses toward the north, estimating the direction, and ignoring the road signs. My beautiful bus gets on the national highway, and then exits. It changes roads six times. This is how I imagine a driver in his death throes: a road that's no longer mastered, the last flight of a huge bumblebee. At each fork in the road, the way gets narrower. On this road, the tree branches lining whip the windows as the bus goes by. They manage to shift the right side-view mirror, folding it against the door. To the east, the sun is beginning to light the sky: a hint of daylight reveals patches of ink.

Where are you going? Where are you taking me? Are you still taking me somewhere?

Basile isn't listening to me. He's breathing heavily. It's clear to me that life is in the process of leaving him, that it's coming up to his mouth or draining into his guts like a ball in a pinball machine, but I can also tell that there's no way that he's going to let himself vomit it up, especially not right in front of me. Everything still takes place cleanly during the emptying process, slowly releasing the breath, the contours, the colors, the fullness, the dimensions, the cavities, the dents . . .

Is he going to dissolve into dust like a forest submerged for too long, resurfacing into the forgotten atmosphere?

But Basile's eyes still tell him that he has to stop now, this is it, please, it doesn't matter where he is, he's arrived. He covers his mouth with his hand, like someone who's going to vomit and would like to avoid doing it in the cabin.

Basile stops my beautiful bus in the spot that he's picked: a rest stop along the road where three cars could park. My beautiful bus takes up the entire lot. There's a short fountain with non-potable water and a push button faucet. A trashcan sits next to it. A dirty hobo is busy rummaging through it. He's surrounded by three plastic bottles full of water. He sits down in the dirt and washes used plastic bags that he has salvaged and emptied out. He takes to this with great care, paying no attention to the newcomers. He puts the bags up to dry, turned inside out and attached by the handle to the lower hanging branches of a walnut tree.

Pshhhh.

A few steps away, there's a Routier, a restaurant and small inn. The building is guarded by a thick curtain of plants. Basile speaks at last:

"I'm going to sleep."

The branches move apart to let him through. They close up behind him.

In my beautiful bus, which all of a sudden appears far more spacious and peaceful, the driver's seat has sunken in and its fabric is tearing. On the ground lie orange peels and tissues. The sun highlights the grime on the windows. I look around in every direction that the horizon offers. And so I find myself alone.

Silence.

I don't know where I am. I no longer know where I departed from nor how long ago. I don't know where I'm going to go home to. I don't know what else I know. I don't know what I'm going to do with what I've seen. I had left in order to uproot myself from a familiar land, to be alone among people who are different from me. But really, why had I left, I who had ruminated Pascal:

I have discovered that all the unhappiness of men arises from one single fact, that they cannot stay quietly in their own chamber.[11]

Since I ended up coming back to Viry, did I ever truly leave? What I wanted to see and hear, what I saw and heard, in my beautiful bus, was it boring or was it monstrous enough? Their unrest. The other can die there . . . I could have killed Odile but I decided not to. However, I did consume all of my characters. I don't have any more left in reserve. All I have left to do now is consume myself in this book, if I knew what role I played in it. When I started, I had stated that my name was usurped on the cover, but it has ended up elbowing its way inside, hopping the fence. I talked about an "I"-character, a hollow narrator, who works with emptiness like a forge bellows or Lao Tzu's jug. Coming back to my stable of departure, am I not in the process of betraying this emptiness, this picket sign of an "I" that should forbid the visible passage of the author onto the page, a smuggler who doesn't know what he's carrying in his chest, or if he himself is the one being carried? Am I not letting myself be sucked in by him? But a first name is a hole in the book, like the emptied

---

[11] Pascal. "Pensée # 139."

heads in daguerreotypes, or Hans Martin's Chinese people in their character façades. J. J. can also poke his head through. But it isn't his head every time. I have hidden myself too much; I have protected myself too much. I had so many questions for Odile, Basile, Hans Martin, and other characters, so many direct questions. I abandoned them in the margins. But now that I have dismissed them, now that I have fled into the landscape to avoid answering them, it's too late.

They also had questions for me, about my homeland, the one that I had left behind, a land where I'm a king like everyone else, a king primarily and simply by lecherousness, king of a few square meters of roofed spaced, and on the same floor a bathroom, a china cabinet, king of the kitchen, king of the little balcony where the laundry hangs to dry during nice weather, kinglet of the wine cellar and the public spaces. I wanted to know, without touching, how they lived or how they loved . . . Perhaps they would have liked it if I had told them about my wife, who is extremely beautiful, who does everything passionately. For me she occupies the entire spectrum of human beauty the moment that I look at her. When she walks, she knocks onlookers over. When she gets up, a fire sparks. Those who watch her go by curse themselves. To smell her perfume is like smelling for the last time. Her hair is a lasso. Her wink is the slice of a dagger and her hand can turn witnesses blind. When she dances, with her back turned, moving away, she kills . . . She doesn't pick up what she has killed. When she swims, she drowns. She can stay under water longer than turtles. Her kisses are liquid gold. She sucks and her mouth is soft like cream. She slips her head under the sheets, and the noises of the city completely die away. When she learns, nothing escapes her. She knows syntax and verse play, old and new, the names of the stars, and geometry. As a baby, she rediscovered Euclid's principles. She can locate every city on the map, rivers, and mountains too. She knows languages. She fishes for trout barehanded and catches larks in flight. She knows the laws of architecture and boldly conceives new forms. She cooks the same way. She has added strings to the lyre. Jurisprudence in the field of inheritance law holds no secrets from her. She's eloquent and keen on logic. If asked the riddle: "What is something? What is half of something? What is nothing?" she's the only one who answers: "The lover is something; the infidel is half of something; the hypocrite is nothing." Having been challenged to show up neither dressed nor naked at a party, she's the only one who would come dressed in a fishing net and spin heads simply by being there, like Salomé dancing. She brings the bread home by playing radio game shows, TV game shows, *Jeopardy*, and word games. In cards, she's worth four kings and four jacks. She crosses words like some people cross their fingers. She's the most secretive, the most obscure, the most difficult, and unparalleled; she demands the greatest transparency and clarity outside of herself. When she has lovers, her ruses are extreme, those ruses to ease pains here and there and to reverse situations that are not in her favor. She knows the virtues of medical plants and knows how to prepare poultices. Her violence is extreme and her pain is immense when it's obvious that I'm in love with someone else. The better to chase them away, she has learned the rules of one-on-one combat. She holds the record in lies: the longest chain. When her face begins to show signs of evildoing, Milady de Merteuil can't hold a candle to her.

I owe everything to her extremes. I surrendered to her supremacy a long time ago. It happened one day when she proved her intelligence in riddles and the solving of impossible contraries to be utterly crushing. I wanted to chase her out of the house, magnanimously begging her to take with her anything and everything from our home that would make her happy. But once again she proved her superiority by lifting me up onto her back and carrying me off to a hotel room to cover me with her melting kisses.

So I had every reason to protect my alliance with her as long as I could. But while on my coach rides through the kingdom, when the peasants who were harvesting the fields, or the land itself, asked me perfidiously who owned me, who owned the hair on my head, this beard, these fingernails, and who owned these deepening wrinkles, I got the feeling that the question was asked mockingly. I couldn't answer, "To me. To me, alone. Carabas, me!" The truth was that I belonged to a woman whose proud admirer I should have been completely happy with being.

This bitterness began gnawing at me. I had betrayed love twice, for a little bit of peace, and to shore up this feeling of lowly pride. Something was thereby stolen from me by the other. I didn't like being half of a couple in the eyes of others. Love is an intimate thing when the couple is a public figure. It's foolish, because the Singular isn't the divine, and the Multiple isn't the devilish, but that's how it was in my mind. It was unbearable to owe my appearance to the couple. The ability to be alone, however, was an illusion.

The third time was even more serious. When she was on the verge of being assassinated by a stranger who wanted to push her out in front of a freight train, I immediately chased after him, following his fresh tracks. The ground was humid and no rain had fallen to wash away the footprints. I followed them carefully all day long and into the night. Amid ants, bits of broken windshields, and candy wrappers, I followed footprints, tire marks, accelerations, tire skids, heel marks pressed deep into the ground ...

I came down on someone somewhat violently, crushing his forearm with an uncontrollably firm grip.

"Could you please let go of me!"

And this is how I got a grip on myself, without really understanding at first, then understanding all too well.

The other person could die, I wanted the other person to die, I was ready to ask for the head of someone else, and be the executioner myself. I flirt with the death of someone else, but only in my mind. When Puss in Boots saves his master from ruin, it's first and foremost to save his own fur and skin, to avoid becoming stew or mittens. But at the end of Basile's fable—here I'm talking about the Napolitano storyteller who also told a pre-Puss in Boots[12]—the pussycat plays dead as a preventive measure and to test the newly rich Cagliuso's feelings. She definitely is enlightened! She leaves, as Basile says in the end, "correndo senza mai voltare la testa" (running without ever looking back). In fable 151 (I.6) by the same Basile, the young girl Zezolla is also forgotten by her debtor and relegated to cooking, adopting the nickname "la gatta Cenerentola," the pussycat of ashes (Cinderella). Why else would she be deemed "pussycat" other than to rhyme with Cagliuso's cat?

What terrible things am I capable of, what does this story reveal about me? Capable of having the Baptist cat's head cut off and serving it to you on a platter.

---

[12] Giambattista Basile, *Lo cunto de li cunti* (1634-1636), also called *Il Pentamerone*, "Cagliuso, fourth pastime of the tenth day," Garzanti, 1986.

This is the only thing that motivated my departure and my surreptitious boarding of my beautiful bus. And I was followed.

I must summarize things more simply. A trip is a cork shot off into the distance. What do I really bring back from it?

I'll buy a notebook and scribble down the events of the trajectory. A trip is a potential book. In order for a book to come of it, I have to leave behind the fiction of my trip on my tiptoes and rediscover the slow walking pace of someone who doesn't have anything left to fear and nothing urgent to attend to, someone who doesn't even have to quicken his step to rediscover what is just as vital as water to him.

I didn't leave. I didn't even believe that I could leave. I made what I already knew move, however little that may be. I will bring something back, though.

It isn't literature that's tragic. Only love is undoubtedly so. Literature is a trivial thing. I'm going to go back home, as long as it's not too late. I'm going to return to my kingdom. Now I remember what my kingdom is like. How does an invented book match up to my own story? And I know what to say to the queen for her to open her arms back up to me and let her hair down for me, for her to wash any bitterness about my crime from her memory. Will I manage? I won't read my book to her. It wouldn't be of any use to us. No need for a mediator. I won't tell her that it wrote itself, as if it were the trip of a shuttle, a schemer, a postman, a sweet meditation, a little passing Jesus, or a lowly, toiling manservant . . . but at some point, I will eventually place the territory itself on her knees. My book is a bus that I have carried along a path.

Night falls. My beautiful bus is an exhausted, dirty, disfigured horse, covered in bumps and dents. No one would be surprised to see it end up at the junkyard.

Basile left the key to the ignition on the dashboard. I should have taken detailed notes on the series of moves he performed throughout this whole trip: turn on the engine, put it into gear, release the hand brake, move forward a few meters . . . another gear . . . Attentiveness is always too muddled. You let your mind get occupied with what you wish later on you had ignored. Fortunately, there's a diagram of the gears drawn on the gearshift.

I sit down behind the wheel. I sit down in the driver's nest. The seat squeaks as it sinks slightly: a little bit of flexibility for the lumbar. It's comfortable enough. More comfortable than the passenger seats were, in any case. I shift the gears, without putting them to work.

I turn around and take a look around the cabin, which I should sweep before leaving. I don't have the broom or the motivation. So much for the orange peels, the beer cans, and apple-juice boxes. I shoot a quick glance at the little hammer used for breaking the windows. It hasn't been used. I adjust the mirrors, the left side-view mirror and the rearview mirror in the middle of the cabin. I stand up to adjust the right side-view mirror. I see the journey gone by again.

Will I be able to handle this hulk? I might bump into signposts and the corners of houses at first . . .

Ah! I remember. That's where you, pshhhh, yes, pshhhh . . .

I sit back down in front of the wheel. What a big wheel!

The blinker? There it is.

The headlights for nighttime . . .

The gas pedal is sensitive. It must feel so powerful!
Alright. Here's the hand brake. Quick!

Well. Now how am I going to start this beautiful bus?

Jacques Jouet was elected to the Oulipo in 1983. He is the author of more than sixty texts in a variety of genres—novels, poetry, plays, literary criticism, and short fiction—including the novels *Mountain R* (part of his La République roman cycle), *Savage*, and *Upstaged*, all published by Dalkey Archive.

Eric Lamb is a literary translator from French. The first installment of his translation of Pierre Grimbert's fantasy series, *The Secret of Ji*, will appear in 2013.

SELECTED DALKEY ARCHIVE PAPERBACKS

FOR A FULL LIST OF PUBLICATIONS, VISIT:
www.dalkeyarchive.com

SELECTED DALKEY ARCHIVE PAPERBACKS

My Life in CIA.
Singular Pleasures.
The Sinking of the Odradek
    Stadium.
Tlooth.
20 Lines a Day.
JOSEPH MCELROY,
    Night Soul and Other Stories.
THOMAS MCGONIGLE,
    Going to Patchogue.
ROBERT L. MCLAUGHLIN, ED., *Innovations:*
    An Anthology of
        Modern & Contemporary Fiction.
ABDELWAHAB MEDDEB, *Talismano.*
HERMAN MELVILLE, *The Confidence-Man.*
AMANDA MICHALOPOULOU, *I'd Like.*
STEVEN MILLHAUSER,
    The Barnum Museum.
    In the Penny Arcade.
RALPH J. MILLS, JR.,
    Essays on Poetry.
MOMUS, *The Book of Jokes.*
CHRISTINE MONTALBETTI, *Western.*
OLIVE MOORE, *Spleen.*
NICHOLAS MOSLEY, *Accident.*
    Assassins.
    Catastrophe Practice.
    Children of Darkness and Light.
    Experience and Religion.
    God's Hazard.
    The Hesperides Tree.
    Hopeful Monsters.
    Imago Bird.
    Impossible Object.
    Inventing God.
    Judith.
    Look at the Dark.
    Natalie Natalia.
    Paradoxes of Peace.
    Serpent.
    Time at War.
    The Uses of Slime Mould:
        Essays of Four Decades.
WARREN MOTTE,
    Fables of the Novel: French Fiction
        since 1990.
    Fiction Now: The French Novel in
        the 21st Century.
    Oulipo: A Primer of Potential
        Literature.
YVES NAVARRE, *Our Share of Time.*
    Sweet Tooth.
DOROTHY NELSON, *In Night's City.*
    Tar and Feathers.
ESHKOL NEVO, *Homesick.*
WILFRIDO D. NOLLEDO, *But for the Lovers.*
FLANN O'BRIEN,
    At Swim-Two-Birds.
    At War.
    The Best of Myles.
    The Dalkey Archive.
    Further Cuttings.
    The Hard Life.
    The Poor Mouth.
    The Third Policeman.
CLAUDE OLLIER, *The Mise-en-Scène.*
    Wert and the Life Without End.
PATRIK OUŘEDNÍK, *Europeana.*
    The Opportune Moment, 1855.
BORIS PAHOR, *Necropolis.*

FERNANDO DEL PASO,
    News from the Empire.
    Palinuro of Mexico.
ROBERT PINGET, *The Inquisitory.*
    Mahu or The Material.
    Trio.
MANUEL PUIG,
    Betrayed by Rita Hayworth.
    The Buenos Aires Affair.
    Heartbreak Tango.
RAYMOND QUENEAU, *The Last Days.*
    Odile.
    Pierrot Mon Ami.
    Saint Glinglin.
ANN QUIN, *Berg.*
    Passages.
    Three.
    Tripticks.
ISHMAEL REED,
    The Free-Lance Pallbearers.
    The Last Days of Louisiana Red.
    Ishmael Reed: The Plays.
    Juice!
    Reckless Eyeballing.
    The Terrible Threes.
    The Terrible Twos.
    Yellow Back Radio Broke-Down.
JOÃO UBALDO RIBEIRO, *House of the*
    Fortunate Buddhas.
JEAN RICARDOU, *Place Names.*
RAINER MARIA RILKE, *The Notebooks of*
    Malte Laurids Brigge.
JULIÁN RÍOS, *The House of Ulysses.*
    Larva: A Midsummer Night's Babel.
    Poundemonium.
    Procession of Shadows.
AUGUSTO ROA BASTOS, *I the Supreme.*
DANIËL ROBBERECHTS,
    Arriving in Avignon.
JEAN ROLIN, *The Explosion of the*
    Radiator Hose.
OLIVIER ROLIN, *Hotel Crystal.*
ALIX CLEO ROUBAUD, *Alix's Journal.*
JACQUES ROUBAUD, *The Form of a*
    City Changes Faster, Alas, Than
        the Human Heart.
    The Great Fire of London.
    Hortense in Exile.
    Hortense Is Abducted.
    The Loop.
    The Plurality of Worlds of Lewis.
    The Princess Hoppy.
    Some Thing Black.
LEON S. ROUDIEZ, *French Fiction Revisited.*
RAYMOND ROUSSEL, *Impressions of Africa.*
VEDRANA RUDAN, *Night.*
STIG SÆTERBAKKEN, *Siamese.*
LYDIE SALVAYRE, *The Company of Ghosts.*
    Everyday Life.
    The Lecture.
    Portrait of the Writer as a
        Domesticated Animal.
    The Power of Flies.
LUIS RAFAEL SÁNCHEZ,
    Macho Camacho's Beat.
SEVERO SARDUY, *Cobra & Maitreya.*
NATHALIE SARRAUTE,
    Do You Hear Them?
    Martereau.
    The Planetarium.

ARNO SCHMIDT, *Collected Novellas.*
  Collected Stories.
  Nobodaddy's Children.
  Two Novels.
ASAF SCHURR, *Motti.*
CHRISTINE SCHUTT, *Nightwork.*
GAIL SCOTT, *My Paris.*
DAMION SEARLS, *What We Were Doing*
    and Where We Were Going.
JUNE AKERS SEESE,
  Is This What Other Women Feel Too?
  What Waiting Really Means.
BERNARD SHARE, *Inish.*
  Transit.
AURELIE SHEEHAN,
  Jack Kerouac Is Pregnant.
VIKTOR SHKLOVSKY, *Bowstring.*
  Knight's Move.
  A Sentimental Journey:
    Memoirs 1917–1922.
  Energy of Delusion: A Book on Plot.
  Literature and Cinematography.
  Theory of Prose.
  Third Factory.
  Zoo, or Letters Not about Love.
CLAUDE SIMON, *The Invitation.*
PIERRE SINIAC, *The Collaborators.*
JOSEF ŠKVORECKÝ, *The Engineer of*
    Human Souls.
GILBERT SORRENTINO,
  Aberration of Starlight.
  Blue Pastoral.
  Crystal Vision.
  Imaginative Qualities of Actual
    Things.
  Mulligan Stew.
  Pack of Lies.
  Red the Fiend.
  The Sky Changes.
  Something Said.
  Splendide-Hôtel.
  Steelwork.
  Under the Shadow.
W. M. SPACKMAN,
  The Complete Fiction.
ANDRZEJ STASIUK, *Fado.*
GERTRUDE STEIN,
  Lucy Church Amiably.
  The Making of Americans.
  A Novel of Thank You.
LARS SVENDSEN, *A Philosophy of Evil.*
PIOTR SZEWC, *Annihilation.*
GONÇALO M. TAVARES, *Jerusalem.*
  Learning to Pray in the Age of
    Technology.
LUCIAN DAN TEODOROVICI,
  Our Circus Presents . . .
STEFAN THEMERSON, *Hobson's Island.*
  The Mystery of the Sardine.
  Tom Harris.
JOHN TOOMEY, *Sleepwalker.*
JEAN-PHILIPPE TOUSSAINT,
  The Bathroom.
  Camera.
  Monsieur.
  Running Away.
  Self-Portrait Abroad.
  Television.
DUMITRU TSEPENEAG,
  Hotel Europa.

  The Necessary Marriage.
  Pigeon Post.
  Vain Art of the Fugue.
ESTHER TUSQUETS, *Stranded.*
DUBRAVKA UGRESIC,
  Lend Me Your Character.
  Thank You for Not Reading.
MATI UNT, *Brecht at Night.*
  Diary of a Blood Donor.
  Things in the Night.
ÁLVARO URIBE AND OLIVIA SEARS, EDS.,
  Best of Contemporary Mexican
    Fiction.
ELOY URROZ, *Friction.*
  The Obstacles.
LUISA VALENZUELA, *Dark Desires and*
    the Others.
  He Who Searches.
MARJA-LIISA VARTIO,
  The Parson's Widow.
PAUL VERHAEGHEN, *Omega Minor.*
BORIS VIAN, *Heartsnatcher.*
LLORENÇ VILLALONGA, *The Dolls' Room.*
ORNELA VORPSI, *The Country Where No*
    One Ever Dies.
AUSTRYN WAINHOUSE, *Hedyphagetica.*
PAUL WEST,
  Words for a Deaf Daughter & Gala.
CURTIS WHITE,
  America's Magic Mountain.
  The Idea of Home.
  Memories of My Father Watching TV.
  Monstrous Possibility: An Invitation
    to Literary Politics.
  Requiem.
DIANE WILLIAMS, *Excitability:*
    Selected Stories.
  Romancer Erector.
DOUGLAS WOOLF, *Wall to Wall.*
  Ya! & John-Juan.
JAY WRIGHT, *Polynomials and Pollen.*
  The Presentable Art of Reading
    Absence.
PHILIP WYLIE, *Generation of Vipers.*
MARGUERITE YOUNG, *Angel in the Forest.*
  Miss MacIntosh, My Darling.
REYOUNG, *Unbabbling.*
VLADO ŽABOT, *The Succubus.*
ZORAN ŽIVKOVIĆ, *Hidden Camera.*
LOUIS ZUKOFSKY, *Collected Fiction.*
SCOTT ZWIREN, *God Head.*